Killing Me Silently

KILLING ME SILENTLY

JW Bella

Library of Congress Cataloging-In-Publication Data

Name: Bella, J.W.
Title: Killing Me Silently

Identifiers:
LCCN: 2021912863

ISBN: 978-1-970135-88-6 (Paperback)
978-1-970135-90-9 (Hardcover)
978-1-970135-91-6 (Ebook)

Published in the United States by Pen2Pad Ink Publishing.

Requests to publish work from this book or to contact the author should be sent to: jwbellawrites@gmail.com

Interior design: Pen2Pad Ink Publishing

DEDICATION

To Jesse Wilson. Thank you for sparking my love for basketball statistics. Rest in love.

To Christopher Jones. Thank you for taking my statistics love to a higher level. Rest in love.

To Kelita Johnson. You told me that I would have to make a decision one day. Today is that day.

To Blaine Morgan. Thank you for igniting my love for old school music.

PRELUDE

"Yo Magic! Your dad! He's on television." Magic looked up from playing Jonas' Nintendo Switch.

"An African-American male is dead after a robbery gone wrong. Sources say that Royalty Calhoune walked into his house at the time the robbery was happening. Mr. Calhoune died from two shots to the chest." Magic froze. He wasn't prepared to see his dad's photo on the 10 PM news. He knew what his dad did was not exactly legal or right. But he provided. He taught. He dreamed. Magic loved that his dad dreamed. Now he would have to be the dream his dad always wanted.

The funeral was a blur. The repast was too. Magic doesn't remember the people he hugged or how many people said I'm sorry to him like they killed his dad. He just remembered being dropped back to his house after everything was over. He walked in and saw remnants of the police department's investigation. Flags. Yellow tape over where his dad was shot. Broken glass from the window the robbers broke into. *I have to go*, Magic told himself. He went into his room. He carefully moved the *Harlem Nights*, *Coming to*

America, and *Trading Places*. Behind the *Trading Places* poster was a safe. He opened it and grabbed the money and gun. He found his red duffel bag and filled the bag with one picture of his parents, the money, his gun, and some clothes. Then, he called his friend Jonas.

"Can you borrow your mom's car?"

"For what?"

"I need you to drop me off at the Greyhound."

"Where the hell you goin'?"

"Bro, are you going to help me or ask 21 questions?"

"Ok. Give me about 20 minutes." Jonas said. They hung up. Magic took a last look around the house that Royalty built. He remembered when his dad sat on the sofa and told him about how he met his mom. He remembered when his dad burned eggs for the first time trying to cook them in the kitchen. He remembered when he finally beat his dad at Madden on the living room sofa. He remembered when his dad showed him how to load a gun in his bedroom. Magic couldn't. He couldn't stay here with these memories. Something needed to change. Jonas honked the horn. He looked back one last time, left the key on the coffee table, and closed the door to his old life.

Chapter 1

Oh I...can hear your footsteps baby...in the daaaark...oh in the dark...

Calia's ears felt Ron Isley's voice caress her body awake. She looked up to see the exposed brick of her loft. It looked like a group of pigs sitting at a table. *I must want barbeque,* she thought. She tried to get up from the bed, but her body was not having that. It was still under the influence of Crown Royal Apple and Cranberry juice plus a massive migraine pounding. She reached for her phone. When she pressed the power button, she looked at the time. 9:34 AM. Then, she saw a text message from Denais.

No casualties last night.

Calia exhaled. Now she could have her orange juice without judgement. Well, once her body got its life together. In the meantime, she went to YouTube to her favorite channel: *Family Business.* Three DJs who are all cousins interview celebrities: Quick Bradley, Jay Trae, and Sunshine.Quick is the asshole: You hate to love him, but you know he tells the truth. Jay Trae tries his best to see things from different points of view. Sometimes, he succeeds. Sometimes, he is a pushover. Sunshine is the female perspective. She holds it down for feminism every day all day. Calia scrolled through the different videos to find the one with Ricky Randall, CEO of Broke Rich Records. She was waiting for this one because of the beef she heard he had with Quick. She found the video and pressed play.

Peace 93.8! You are here with Quick, Jay Trae, and Sunshine here on the Family Business. Today's guest is BrokeRich's CEO Ricky Randall! How are you, sir?" Jay Trae asked.

"I'm ok with you and Sunshine. My problem is with this bitch ass ho here." Ricky responded pointing at Quick. Quick gave this fake innocent shock look.

"What I did?" Quick said with a high-pitched voice.

"You know what the fuck you did!" Ricky said.

"You right. I do. But truth is truth. Your label would be nothing without Darren Grey. Pissing him off was the stupidest thing you could do. And you apparently have no one in your life that can be honest with you because now you think you can rap! You need some NO people in your life." Quick said without a blink of an eye.

"Look...Darren knew better than to think he could take my spot. I run this shit and I been runnin' this shit for over 20 years! Can't nobody do this better than me!" Ricky responded.

"Ok look," Sunshine started, "First, both of you

are going to stop all this damn hollering. Second, if you don't like Quick obviously you will not like the rest of us because, like it or not, we family. Now you can continue this interview and try to come to some type of understanding, or you can get the hell out." Sunshine's face looked like a black momma in a church about to beat the hell out of her two kids.

"So what? All y'all gone gang up on me?" Ricky asked.

"No. Quick can fight for himself. But this interview is about how you have new artists on your squad. Whatever beef you got with my cousin... deal with that on your own time." Sunshine responded.

"Hell nah! Y'all need to put some respect on my name! Fuck this shit. I'm outta here mane!" Ricky and all 13 members of his crew got up and left the studio. Quick started laughing. Jay's mouth flew open, and Sunshine shook her head. Calia started cracking up on her bed.

"Well I guess that was a bust. You are listening to Peace93.8 with Quick, Jay Trae, and Sunshine on the *Family Business.* We'll be back without Ricky and his crew." The video ended. Calia put her phone down and slowly raised up from her bed. She chuckled at how childish grown men could be. And as much as she didn't like Ricky, she applauded in her head his ability to speak his mind with such ease. He could get angry and frustrated and say something... even if he caught hell and highwater for it. She wished she could do the same.

CHAPTER 2

Orcon passed by his alma mater, James Madison High School. He pulled into the parking lot, and there it was. The bullet holes were still in the side of the building from when Jessla's ex-boyfriend got upset because Magic was taking her to homecoming. He smiled. His dad taught him how to fight and how to disarm someone who is holding a gun. "What kinda Rush Hour shit you just did?" Justin responded after Magic had a gun pointed to his face. "The kind that still has your girl. Good night Justin." He watched Justin get in his car and drive off. The next Monday at school, Justin just passed by Magic while Jessla was laughing and holding Magic's waist.

His dad's words always brought him comfort. "You don't always have to shoot. You just need to require respect...with the intention to shoot by any means necessary." *By any means necessary,* Orcon said to himself as he backed out of the high school parking lot and turned back onto MLK Boulevard. He continued his trek through his old neighborhood by turning right on Meadows and heading to the MLK Child Care center. Across the street was his old apartment he had for his one year as a Madison HS student. The house was now condemned like most of the neighborhood in Oak Cliff. He continued driving to get back on MLK and head to his office in Downtown Dallas. Orcon was now the Senior Vice President of Operations for the Dallas Leopards Basketball Team. It was a 20-year plight to this position, and Orcon took pride that he was one of the many African Americans in leadership positions for such a great team. One of his next projects is to have the team members and staff give back to Oak Cliff as much as the community gave him and gave the team during each of their 4 back to back championships. He was pulling up to the Leopards headquarters and headed into the office when his phone rang.

"Hey Mama Janice! Everything ok?" He asked.

"Baby...you may want to come say goodbye to Cade." she said solemnly.

"I'm on my way." Orcon sped out of the headquarters driveway and made his way to Highland Park Estates.

It took a while for Orcon to get used to big city life after leaving his hometown. Dallas was one of the biggest cities in the state of Texas, and it had 4.3 million people in its population to prove it. Highways crossed every kind of way and getting off on the wrong exit could have you in the hood with the homeless or among the uppity negroes with sparkling pools and 3 to 4 dogs to walk on their jogs. Orcon sped off the ramp from Highway 75 and headed to the Boulder Estates. They lived about 1 mile from Southern Methodist University's football stadium on 3 acres of city land. Orcon was like a son to them, so the guards waved him into the gates of the estate. He drove in the parking circle in the front of their plantation-style mansion painted a sunny tan instead of the typical white. He walked into the house and saw Rosie, their usually upbeat housekeeper.

"He's in his room." she said sniffling. Cade went up the stairs two by two and opened the last door on the left. He immediately saw Janice and hugged her.

"Hey Mama Bear." Orcon hugged Janice.

"Hey my baby. I'm glad you made it."

"How long does he have?"

"Doctors said any time now. He's been waiting on you." He left Janice and went to the bed.

"Hey O." Cade said quietly.

"How are you feeling?" Orcon asked.

"Ready."

"Well I should have seen that coming." Orcon chuckled.

"Look...I've lived my life. Praised my God. Made my money. Married my honey. And along the way made a lot of racist folks mad. I'm good. Don't worry about me."

"True. But...I just...thank you. Thank you for everything you've done for me. Your trust. Your hell and high-water," Orcon chuckled while a couple of tears made it through the barrier of his left eye. "I'm going to miss you."

"Negro my body will be gone. I'm always with you," Cade started coughing. "And I'm leaving my team in good hands."

"I don't think we are ready for Mama Janice."

"Janice wants to enjoy games. She doesn't want to have to choke someone for not having common sense. We leaving it to you." Cade said. Orcon stopped breathing and stared at Cade. "O? O. Breathe boy!" Orcon exhaled.

"Me? The team?" Orcon asked.

"You have spent 20 years with us. You saw us at 4 and 19 and you've seen us win championships. There is no one more qualified for this than you." Cade said softly. Orcon hugged Cade with all his might.

"Thank you...I...I... just...thank you!" Orcon exclaimed.

"Thank YOU. Janice? Come here, baby." Cade called his wife. She sat on the other side of the bed. They reminisced on multiple memories from Orcon's graduation from University of Texas at Dallas to the last championship when they beat the Chicago Bulls. They talked and talked until Cade Kente Boulder took his last breath at 1:13 AM.

Chapter 3

"At this time, we ask for everyone to join us in a moment of silence in honor of Mr. Cade Boulder, past owner of the Dallas Leopards who passed away this past week. We thank him and his wife Janice for the many years they have led the Leopards organization."

The entire American Airlines Arena went silent as a montage of pictures of Cade appeared on every single screen. Shades of purple and gold lit every nook and cranny of the court in honor of Mr. Boulder's favorite colors and Greek organization.

"Thank you. In honor of Mr. Boulder, tonight's jerseys will be his favorite colors. After the game, the jerseys will be signed and donated to Mr. Boulder's favorite non-profit: George's Child. This organization raises funds for children whose parents were victims of police brutality. Now let's get ready for some basket baaaaaaallllll!"

That was Calia's cue. She put on her headphones. J Dilla's heavy bass started to seep into her brain cells. She was ready to work. It was this same weird style of work that got her to this level of basketball statistics. She started doing stats in the 9th grade at Ranchview

High School when she needed a reason to meet boys from other schools. Eventually, she started paying more attention to the game than dudes (but she had no problem with looking at the dudes either).

Her coach recommended her to Daniel Kepler and Blacktop Numbers, an organization dedicated to doing stats for grassroots and adolescent basketball. Kepler took her under her wing with stats, and she continued to fly through Math classes in school like a falcon. She received a Math scholarship to Texas A & M and graduated with honors at 22 with a bachelor's degree. By that time, she led the training department of Blacktop Numbers where she taught high schoolers how to be just as awesome with numbers as she was. She was at a tournament when Drame Jones tapped her on the shoulder during her break.

“Are you Calia?”

“Who wants to know?”

“Me. My name is Drame. I’m in charge of stats and numbers for the Dallas Leopards. Daniel said I could find you here.”

“The Dallas Leopards? With Colton Reese who has 12.9 rebounds, 21.9 points, and 5 blocks per game?”

“Damn. You just know that for the sake of knowing?”

“It’s really...really nice to meet you. Sorry for the attitude. I’ve been doing 5 games straight.”

“No... No... Attitude is good. It’s needed in this

business sometimes. I have a proposition for you." That proposition turned into her becoming the lead statistician for the Dallas Leopards team. She knows that she is in a male dominated business, and she could care less. Her brain and numbers make love anytime she watches teams go up and down a court. If the headphones are on, nothing else matters.

Halftime came before Calia blinked. She finished up her last report, printed it, and handed it over to Drame to pass to the coaches. She was about to get up and do her game stretch when the announcer began his halftime spill.

"Before we begin our halftime revelry, we want to welcome the new owner of the Dallas Leopards. Please give it up for Mr. Orcon Jessley!" Calia's eyes were locked on a tall and handsome gentleman coming onto the court. His dark suit complemented his caramel complexion and greenish brown eyes. He waved to the crowd. *Damn,* Calia said. *I love my job.*

"Drame, who is that?" she asked.

"Orcon? He's been with the Leopards since he was like 18 years old. Worked his way up to being Senior VP. Guess now he's the owner and our new boss. Cool dude when he wants to be." Drame responded.

"Hmmm...Ok. I'm going for my walk. I got 9 minutes." Calia walked away from the table and headed toward the Home Team locker room entrance. She always took a couple minutes away from the table and the crowd and the craziness to reset before she had to go back in and focus. She didn't talk to people.

Always looked at the ground. She just wanted time to not have numbers running her head. She heard the one-minute buzzer and ran back to her table and headphones.

She ran back to her table, put her headphones back on, and got back into the zone. Sometimes, she pinched herself to be in her dream job. Her mom was always good with numbers and had this weird knack for knowing how to count days on a calendar without even thinking. Calia wondered sometimes if her mom would possess her body as she took stats. There were games when she didn't remember any big dunks or big plays that would happen, but they were in her stats. Either way, she wished her mom was here to talk to.

Calia blinked again, and the Leopards won 101-93 against the New Orleans Pelicans. She finished her final reports, submitted her work to Drame, and headed to the Home Team entrance so she could go home. She hoped she could make it to the parking lot without running into...

"Calia...Calia...Calia...my queen." *Shit,* she thought. She knew that voice too well.

"Colton. Hi. Sup?" she asked looking up to her 6-foot 7 stature. She used to admire Colton and his athletic ability. After getting to know him, however, she realized just how much of an ass he really is.

"Looking good...as always." Colton responded.

"I know. That's expectation. How may I help you?"

"What were my stats tonight?"

"You had 21 points, 4 rebounds, and 6 assists."

"I love how you can just rattle that off. It's so...sexy."

"Your thots don't know how to count?" She smirked.

"Not like you. C'mon Cal...We won tonight. We gotta celebrate."

"We don't have to do anything. Enjoy your night Colton." Colton reached out and grabbed her arms. Calia immediately looked down at her arm then up at Colton with the most sinister eyes. He removed his hand immediately.

"Look. Just a drink. That's all I'm asking. One drink."

"I'm good, Mr. Reese," Calia looked behind him. "It seems like you already have people to celebrate with." She looked behind him to see a sea of ladies waiting and screaming for Colton. "Good night, sir." Calia walked off and headed to her car. She was ready to party and blow off some steam as far away from Colton as possible.

CHAPTER 4

"Dad?" Calia said as she walked in her dad's house.

"I'm in the kitchen!" He shouted. She took her shoes off, put her keys down, and headed to the kitchen.

"Ready?" She asked.

"Yeah. Can you help me with some of these things?"

She picked up the biscuits and put them on the table next to the sweet potatoes and grilled chicken. Calia picked up her dad's ability to cook. That's the only thing she can really appreciate from him now. These Sunday dinners started with her mom. Rachel LaCaze would talk about how it was something that black families did in order to keep some type of normalcy and community during riots, protests, and civil rights. "If we can sit at the table, love will meet us there." Rachel would say. When she died, Calia was seven years old. Since then, Calia and her dad have had Sunday dinners as a way of staying connected with their busy work schedules. After Jayden sat the wine glasses on the table, he grabbed Calia's hand. "Can you bless the food please?" He asked.

"Father, we thank you for the food and the hands that prepared it. Bless it so that it is nourishing to our minds, bodies, and souls. Amen."

"Amen." Jayden repeated. They started to fix their plates and eat in silence. Their Sunday dinners were silent since Calia was in the 9th grade. They had a huge fight that caused them not to talk for about 2 weeks. They eventually apologized, but the topic of the conversation still lingers in Calia's mind.

"How was the game?" Jayden asked, breaking the silence.

"Good." Calia responded.

"I... I watched it. I tried to look for you, but I couldn't see you."

"I sit on the opposite side from the benches."

"Oh right. My mistake." They went back to eating.

"You talked to Denais lately?"

"Yep."

"Well, how is she?"

"Good."

"Oh. Well good." Silence returned.

"You talked to your side of the family?" Calia asked with a smirk on her face.

"No. You already know that." Jayden retorted.

"And why is that?"

"Because... I don't have a reason to do so."

Calia stopped. Then, she put her fork down, wiped her mouth, and looked up. "Really? You don't?"

"Calia...please don't start this. Can we just eat in peace?"

"Sure." She paused. "By the way, I had an episode."

This time Jayden put down his fork, wiped his mouth, and looked up.

"When?!" He asked.

"A couple of nights ago. No one died this time. I didn't end up in the hospital...this time."

"Calia...you have to learn how to contr--"

"Control?" Calia cut him off. "How in the hell am I going to do that? The one person who can teach me pretends like it doesn't exist!"

"I'm not pretending." Jayden said sternly.

"So... this not acknowledging or discussing of it...this...this is not pretending?"

"Calia. You have the ability to control it if you want to."

"Oh, like you did. Ignoring is not the same as pretending."

"I'm not pretending, Calia."

"Then what are you doing?! No one died...this

time. I don't know what may happen the next time! The only reason it doesn't happen now is because I got this shit from you!"

Jayden stood up. "Hold the fuck on now! I am still your father. Sit cho' little ass down and take that profanity out of your mouth at me." Calia looked back down at her plate.

"I...I am sorry." She said quietly. She put her napkin on the table, backed away from the table, and headed for the door.

"One day...you don't want me to be in jail or dead when you try to help." Calia grabbed her keys and left the house.

She hopped in her car and sat in silence. She inhaled and exhaled. She needed a drive. Being around people right now is not safe for anyone. She needed a trek by White Rock Lake to refocus herself.

The parking lot next to the Arboretum was empty. She parked her car, put her windows down, and reclined her seat. Roberta Flack's version of "Killing Me Softly" mixed with the chirps of birds flying by as she heard waves crash. *This was my fault,* she said. *I knew bringing that up would hit a nerve. But I need to know. I need to know how to control this before it gets worse.* She closed her eyes and listened to Roberta repeat the chorus.

Strummin' my pain with his fingers...
Singin' my life with his words...
Killin' me softly with his song...

Killin' me softly with his song tellin' my whole life with his words...

Killin' me...softly...with his sooooong...

CHAPTER 5

After being a member of the Dallas community for over 20 years...no....no... That's too obvious, Orcon said to himself. *I've been fortunate to live, breathe, and experience Dallas for over 20 years...yeah...there it is.* He scratched out the old sentence on his note card and added the new one. No matter how many times he had to speak in front of a crowd, Orcon always found himself nervous. It was like 10th grade speech class with Mrs. Martinez all over again, and that woman did not play when it came to Public Speaking. She would be happy at the purpose of this speech. He was the keynote speaker to the Independent Party Luncheon being held at the Hilton Anatole Hotel. She always said he was going to make big moves, but she was never sure if it was to become a CEO of a company or a CEO of a street pharmacist company. Either way, he had a way with people and words.

"Big O!" A voice belted from behind his back said. Orcon turned around.

"Really? Big O? Here?"

"Don't act like I'm going to change because of all of these sadiddy black, brown, and white people. I'm consistent. You ready?"

"Yeah. I'm ready to get this off my chest. I just wish Cade was here. I can hear him now. 'Boy we got stuff to do. Say what cha gotta say so I can eat!'" Orcon chuckled.

"Yep. Mr. B never liked staying at these types of functions for long. You wanna grab a drink afterwards and meet at Cajun Cigar? It's Ladies Night." Maze asked.

"We'll see how this goes first. I can't drink anything if I don't get what I want from these people."

Heels clicked on the floor. "Mr. Jessley? They are ready for you." the organizer of the event stated.

"Alright," Orcon replied. "Let's do this." He followed her to the door.

"Please welcome our Keynote Speaker, the newly appointed CEO and General Manager of the Dallas Leopards Basketball Team, Mr. Orcon Jessley!" Orcon opened the door to see a sea of people stand up and clap as he made his way to the podium. He flashed his million-dollar smile and waved like he was Barack Obama boarding the Air Force One Jet. He shook the hand of Mel, the man who did his introduction. Then, he placed his note cards on the podium and closed his eyes. *Dad, wherever you are, be my guide. Amen.* He said to himself.

"Thank you, Mel, for that awesome introduction. I feel like I can conquer the world now. You must have received pointers from Steve Harvey, huh?" The crowd chuckled. "Have a seat, please. I'm going to be here for a while. First, thank you for this opportunity. It is amazing to see so many people who are a part of this Dallas community come together in order to build a better city with a great heart. I've been fortunate to live, breathe, and experience Dallas for the last 20 years of my life. I've seen the struggle of Oak Cliff, the creativity of the Arts District, the eccentricity of the Oak Lawn Avenue, the musicality of Deep Ellum, and the flavor that all of our surrounding cities add to make this place an exceptional place to live. I'm not going to stand here and pretend that all my experiences have been perfect. I worked very hard from being an intern for the Dallas Leopards organization to where I am now. However, each moment of mountains and valleys made me better. They helped me to learn from my mistakes. They encouraged me to embrace change instead of being afraid of it. I do not regret a single moment, and neither should you. Whatever it is that has tried to harm you or keep you from victory was just a set up for your greatness. Looking out into this small part of the Dallas family, I see greatness at each table. I want to continue helping this city become the best it can be in business, creativity, and lifestyle. That is why I am announcing that I am running to be the next Mayor of Dallas. I hope, with your support, that we all can make Dallas bigger and better!"

The crowd erupted into applause. Orcon looked down and closed his eyes. *Thank you, Dad,* he said to himself. He looked up and flashed his million-dollar smile. Mel tapped him on the shoulder.

"Son...I think you have the support you need." Mel said. Orcon exhaled. He was ready for the next set of mountains and valleys to come.

Maze stood up and clapped with the rest of his table. He was proud of Orcon's speech and his bravery. He watched Orcon grow up in the Dallas Leopards organization and even surpass him to become CEO. He saw this young black man struggle from pain to progress. He never understood what motivated Orcon, but he wished he had the same diligence. He watched as Orcon went around shaking hands and hugging people around the room. When Orcon finally made it to his table, he did his secret handshake with Orcon and smiled.

"Watch dog?" Maze asked.

"Bow Wow." Orcon replied.

CHAPTER 6

The line for Sandaga813 flowed down the sidewalk as people patiently waited to get in. Calia and Denais giggled as they saw women wobbling left and right in 5-inch stilettos they could barely walk in. After many glorious nights of partying in and around the Dallas area, Calia and Denais knew that comfortable was way more important than fashionable. If heels were important to having fun and gaining the attention of attractive gentlemen, they rather get drinks from men who made Jerome from Martin look like *GQ* Model of the Year.

"Southern Hummingbird was wayyyyyy better than Charlene." Calia argued.

"Uh...no. Charlene was Tweet's truth." Denais countered. It never failed. They always found some way to argue about music that was considered "Old School". Denais was Calia's pusher into the music realm since they were kids. She was also the only member on Mom's side of the family she could tolerate for longer than 33 seconds. They continued to argue over the best album by Tweet until their IDs were checked and they were in the club. J Dilla's "So

Far To Go" featuring Common and D'Angelo caressed their ear drums as they entered the crowded palace for all things soul. They immediately went to the bar to order drinks and start a tab. Calia stuck to her traditional Crown Royal Apple and Cranberry Juice. Denais sipped her Amaretto Sour with pride. They were able to find seats on the far wall where they could "people watch": Observe random people and create stories about who they were and their purpose for being in the club.

"He look like a Frank," Calia started. "He paints houses for a living, but he tells his girls he's an architect."

"He don't look like he can spell architect." Denais responded.

"The girls he date don't ask him too. They probably can't spell it either." Calia answered. They burst into laughter making everyone else look at them for a second before going back to what they were doing.

"Aw shit. The hell he doin' here?" Calia asked out loud. A familiar 6-foot 7 stature started making his way toward her. Multiple color lights bounced off his high-top fade perfectly cut around his square face. He complemented his dark blue quarter sleeve V-neck with a simple gold chain. As he came closer, he revealed dark blue jeans and Blue Retro Air Jordan's on his feet. The crowd parted for him as he did handshakes with some people and hugs with others. His eyes may have veered off for a second, but his focus was on Calia.

"Greetings Ladies." Colton said.

"Well hello. How are you?" Denais answered.

"Good." He moved his attention to Calia. "How we doin' tonight, Lady?"

"Colton." Calia responded. She took a huge gulp of her drink.

"She is so rude," Denais interrupted, "I'm Denais. Calia's cousin."

"Nice to meet you. Seems like beauty runs all over this family." Colton replied, reaching out to shake Denais' hand.

"Yep. It pretty much does." Denais replied.

"How may I help you tonight, sir? I'm off the clock." Calia asked.

"A dance would help get rid of me....with you." Colton answered.

"I don't want to lose my seat." Calia responded.

"Oh, I can help with that," Denais said, "You go. Nobody will take your seat." Calia gave her the stare of death as if to say *you are not helping, D!* Denais recognized the look, but she didn't care. "Go ahead. I'll watch your drink."

Calia hung her head and got up. Colton took her hand and guided her to the dance floor. Common and Mary J. Blige's "Come Close" started to play. Colton swung Calia around slowly until she was facing him. She had no choice but to look up at his immaculately shaved beard under his dreamy lips. She placed her arms around his neck and did her best to look to the left and right of him while Common's rap was being sung by almost everyone on the dance floor. "Did you do this on purpose?" She asked Colton.

"Do what?" Colton asked.

"Request this song."

"No. Just lucky I guess. Why you keep pretending like this shouldn't happen?"

"This?"

"Yes! Me. You."

"Because it's not. I get it. You like me as the chase. But I'm not what you need in your life."

"I think you are."

"Why is that? You got girls throwing panties and pussy at yo' ass."

"Well...you are smart. You know what you want. You are not looking for me as a come up. You already have your own."

"True," Calia agreed, "Appreciate the compliments. But...I'm good. Not ready for relationships right now. Plus, I'm not in the mood to beat a bitch while you on the road and shit. I'm not that strong."

"Well...does it have to be a relationship? Can we just...chill?"

"Nope. I like my low body count. I'm not trying to

be in the Guinness World Record Book," Calia moved her hands away from Colton's neck and grabbed his face, "But...thank you for the dance." She kissed his cheek. "Enjoy your night. I think you have some people who want your attention." She looked to her left at all the ladies looking at her with daggers in her eyes. Then, she walked back to her spot near her cousin.

"That is a gorgeous man, Cal." Denais replied, giving Calia her drink.

"I know. But the personality doesn't match the outside. I'm good. When is Buffalo Black performing?" Calia responded.

"I think he starts in a couple of minutes. I'm about to lose my mind on his song 'Wolves'."

"You always do. We should probably move toward the stage while no one is really paying attention." They finished their drinks and moved toward the stage. They found a spot close to the stage to see him without squinting but not close enough to smell his sweat and deodorant. Once they had the spot-on lock, they continued dancing to add the great hits the DJ was playing. Sometimes they laughed and mingled with other people who were dancing, but they were in their own little bubble for most of the time.

"Are y'all ready for the main event?!" The DJ announced. The crowd went crazy in anticipation.

"We not gone hold y'all in suspense. Ladies and Gentlemen...please welcome...Buffalo Black!"

Everyone rushed the stage. Calia and Denais felt like a huge sound wave pushed them closer to the edge of the stage. They held their spot and were grateful they moved when they did. When the wave finished, Calia and Denais were not in the spot they started. Two new people somehow made their way in front of them that were not there before.

"Excuse me?" Calia asked as respectfully as she could, "You are in our spot."

"I don't see your name anywhere." The girl responded.

"Last time I checked, your name wasn't here either. Now move." Denais said aggressively.

"Me and Mickey ain't moving nowhere." The girl's friend responded. Denais looked at Calia's face. She knew that face.

"I said MOVE before I do it for you." Denais answered.

"Bitch I'm not moving anywhere!" Mickey responded. Denais looked at Calia. Her head was down. She was stone still. She touched Calia. Her body was warm.

"Oh shit! Cal! Calia! Calia chill out!" Denais tried to get through to Calia. It wasn't working. Calia looked up. Her face was completely still. She said absolutely nothing. She just looked at one of the girls. Then, her look shot to the left of her. Another girl turned around to look at the first people who took Calia and Denais' spot.

"The fuck you said about me, Bitch?" The girl asked.

"I said, you Grover looking mother fucker!" Mickey responded.

"I know you ain't talking Kermit the Frog. How much fuckin' tea you drank to have that stank ass breath?!"

"Enough for your nasty ass to bathe in BITCH!"

Mickey's right fist connected with the girl's left cheek. The girl stumbled back and touched her face. Then, she grabbed Mickey's hair and threw her to the ground. Mickey's head bashed against the concrete floor, but it didn't even phase her. She reached up and tied the girl's shirt around her fist. The girl fell on top of her and she flipped her onto the concrete floor. Then, a flurry of Mickey's fists went left and right on the girl's face.

"Is this what you want? Huh?! Is this what you want?" Mickey kept repeating. Everyone in the crowd had their phones out recording the girls tumbling and tussling in the crowd.

"Yo! Security! We need help over here!" Buffalo Black shouted from the stage. It took a while, but security was able to finally make it to the fight and break it up. Shoes were gone. Weave was all over the floor.

"What happened to her?" One security guard said as he looked at Calia passed out on the floor.

CHAPTER 7

Sunlight beamed across the long mahogany table in the executive conference. Orcon always came in an hour before everyone else just because. Plus, the downtown Dallas skyline was immaculate. He could see clearly to the jogging paths near the Margaret Hunt Hill Bridge. People looked like raisins with brightly colored clothing running and walking. His eyes started to move in to see Interstate 35 carrying cars, trucks, and bad drivers north and south of Downtown. *I know, huh Dad?* Orcon said to himself. *I can't believe it either*.

"I swear you daydream more than me in Geometry class in high school." Maze said, interrupting the peace.

"How did you, the Chief Financial Officer of the Dallas Leopards Basketball Organization, daydream in a math class?" Orcon asked.

"If you had the teacher I had, you would understand. She talked like the dude from the Clear Eyes commercial."

"Ouch. I would have fallen asleep too."

"Fallen asleep on who?" Jordan McAfee asked as he walked into the conference room.

"His Geometry teacher." Orcon said, pointing to Maze.

"You had one of those teachers, too?" Jordan asked.

"Mine was my World Geography Teacher. All he wanted to talk about was being the Volunteer Fire Fighter for his town."

"You can volunteer to do that? Who does that without being paid?" Maze asked.

"Same question I would ask," Orcon replied, "How's it going, Coach?"

"I'm here. That's all I got for now." Jordan replied, adjusting his seat. The rest of the executive team started to pour in for their 1:30 PM meeting. They knew Orcon started his meetings one minute early on purpose. To be on time was to be late.

"Good afternoon. Let's get started. Jorge, can you give us an update on possible trades?"

"Yep. Afternoon everyone. I had the chance to go to Iowa to see Tristan Zinc. His physical quality is amazing even after his surgery. I would definitely consider him for the Leopards squad."

"But would Carlan be willing to give him up? He's only been there for two years, and they have gone to the playoffs since he's been there." Dane Alltura, the Leopards' consultant, asked.

“It may be hard to get him but not impossible. Asiah can explain that more.” Jorge replied.

“Jorge’s right. Carlan doesn’t have the financial stability to satisfy Tristan’s salary demands. Zinc’s going to walk. From what I’ve seen from Maze, you all may be able to catch him at a steal...if you play your numbers right.” Asiah responded.

“Before I get to that, Drame, what are his stats looking like?” Orcon asked.

“According to my research, he makes 22 points per game, 7 offensive rebounds, 10 defensive rebounds, and 5 assist per game. That’s a lot for someone his size.” Drame explained.

“Hmm...Ok. You're right. Maze, can we afford it?” Orcon asked.

“I don’t know...if we do, we may be taking away from one of our franchise players. I don’t think that's a good move.” Maze responded.

“We have a couple that need a new parking lot anyway. They are getting stale playing with me. Stout can go.” Jordan responded.

“Coach...,” Asiah replied, “Let it go, please.”

“Hell no I’m not letting it go! He had the nerve to correct me in front of my own team and--”

“Jordan...I know you are upset, but you and I can discuss that at another time.” Orcon interrupted. “Maze, work with Asiah to give me a complete report of what is available. I want it on my desk by Friday at

Noon."

Maze exhaled. "Okay." He responded.

"Thank you everyone for your input. We'll revisit this on Monday. I want to move on this by Wednesday of next week. I don't need any leaks or stupidity on social media throwing bugs into this plan. My next topic is probably easier to digest. I notice a lot of protesting and issues with police brutality lately due to the killing of Ivarius Duncan. As a black man, I find it very hard to stand by and do nothing. In a couple of days, the team will receive our bonus as a result of making it to the semi-finals last year. I am making the executive decision to donate that to our new non-profit "I Know I Can". This will go towards teaching young black men and women more about their heritage, their culture, and the importance of their lives. While I cannot stop the police department from killing people of color yet, I'm hoping that people will follow our lead toward the cause." Orcon finished and looked around the table to head nods and smiles...except from one person.

"Excuse me?" Maze interjected.

"What's the problem?" Orcon asked.

"How are you going to make a financial decision without discussing it with me? How do you know all of us want to donate to that cause?!" Maze shouted.

Orcon paused before responding. "Ladies and Gentlemen, I apologize but I need to speak with Mr. Seager in private. Thank you for your time." Everyone left the conference room except for Maze and Orcon.

Once the door was closed, Orcon sat down, crossed his left leg over his right, and sat back in his chair with his hands on his lap.

"First...what we don't do is scream like I'm a damn kid," Orcon started. "So before we continue this conversation...I highly advise both of us take a minute to--"

"I'm not taking a minute for shit, Jessley!" Maze interrupted. "This is bullshit! We earned those bonuses! Why can't we have the money?!"

Orcon sat silently and just stared at Maze.

"Answer me!" Maze screamed. Orcon continued to stare. Maze sat down and placed his hands flat on the conference table.

"Orcon...I... I just don't think you are thinking about how this may affect everyone." Maze said calmly.

"What am I not thinking about?" Orcon said calmly.

"You don't know what people had planned for that money. It's...it's not right to dismiss their feelings."

"You are right. Consideration is important. However, if I want to help young black men fight a system that is rigged against them, I will. And I will do it by any means necessary. You don't have to like my decision. But...as the person who works under me...you will respect it. I am not changing my mind. My decision is final. Let me know when the money comes in and when it is given to our Community Relations Advisor." Orcon gathered his things and walked out of the conference room.

Maze slumped in his chair. The sunlight looked like it was burning a hole in the table. He focused on it so much to where he imagined smoke rising like a signal for help. *This is some bullshit,* Maze said to himself. He took out his phone, looked for a number, and dialed it.

"Chance. We need to talk." Maze said firmly.

CHAPTER 8

Tap dancing. Somebody was tap-dancing on Calia's brain, and she couldn't get them to stop. She put her right hand over her closed eyes in hopes of quelling the dancing, but it was in vain. Then, her phone made it worse with a single "ding".

You got 50 minutes. Wash yo' ass.

She tried to get up, but the tap-dancing continued. She started feeling on the side of her bed for her nightstand. She felt something cold. Orange Juice! She grabbed the juice and guzzled it as fast as she could without choking. The tap-dancing started to minimize slowly to nothing. She opened her eyes to find herself in her same clothes from last night at the concert. She got up and showered. She tried to remember what happened, but all she remembered was some chick moving in front of her. She prayed that no one died this time.

A rhythmic beat rattled her front door. "Open this door! I've seen you naked already!"

"Denais. How lovely of you to share that information with the neighborhood." Calia said.

"I'm sure they have done worse." Denais answered plopping on the sofa.

"What happened last night?" Calia asked.

"No one died, but they ended up calling an ambulance for those chicks. I had some help this time getting you to the car."

"This is really starting to piss me off."

"Did you talk to your Dad or is he still being an a-hole about it?"

"We never made it that far in the conversation before I left. I have to figure out who can help me."

Denais hugged Calia. "I know sweetie. Auntie Rachel would have definitely taught you what you needed to know if she had powers."

"I know," Calia started, "I'm just tired. I'm tired of always ending up in this weird space between killer and citizen. I didn't ask for these abilities! I didn't ask for this family!"

"First off, you don't need to scream. I'm right here. Second, none of us had a choice, but that doesn't stop us from living our best lives. So you can kill the wanna be 16-year-old act and figure out how you are going to change your situation."

Calia exhaled. "You're right. I know you right. So let me think. Dad will not help. But maybe his dad will."

"Ok...we getting somewhere. Can your dad give you

his contact information?"

"That's a hell no. If I even say something close to "grandpa", Jayden loses it. What about your side?"

"You have more luck squeezing a quarter out of the dad from Everybody Hates Chris."

"I guess I'm on my own for this one."

"Can I help with anything?"

"Nah...This one is on me to figure out. But thanks anyway. Now why did you come here? I know it wasn't to see me naked."

"Of course not. I came to introduce you to Syreeta Wright. This chick is a singing beast! She sang with Stevie Wonder."

"So did Minnie Riperton. What's so special about her?"

"She married Stevie."

"For real? But...he can't..."

"Look just because he can't see doesn't mean he can't do grown people things. Now shut up and listen to the song." Denais hit play and an emotional clavinet filled the speakers of Calia's living room. Calia closed her eyes. She tried to envision what Syreeta looked like based on her voice. Thin. Brown chocolate skin. Long black relaxed hair. Emphatic brown eyes accented by long eyelashes. She could see Stevie's head moving from left to right listening to Syreeta hug the microphone with her soprano voice. Calia sunk back into her sofa as Syreeta repeated the chorus:

She.......is leavin'.......hoooooome...

She is leaving home after living alone for so many years...

Denais always knew how to pick on time songs. It was time for Calia to leave home if she wanted help.

CHAPTER 9

"I promise...I...I can have it for you by this Friday." Maze said desperately.

"You said that the last time Maze. And I still haven't received my money."

"But that wasn't my fault. I had to wait. But now I'm certain we are getting this bonus. Friday. I can do Friday."

The man on the phone exhales loudly. "Friday. If I do not see my money Friday, yo' ass is mine Saturday." Click. Maze dropped the phone from his ear and exhaled. He had until Friday to pay off his gambling debt. He knew the bonus would come in on Wednesday, but he wanted a couple of days to figure out how to get The Leopards organization out of this non-profit idea. He felt bad for little black kids, but Maze liked his life a little more than them. *They could wait,* he thought to himself. He poured his usual Hennessey about a ½ inch away from the brim of his drinking cup. Then, he took sips as he paced. *Orcon is clearly out of his mind,* Maze continued to think. *We can help them fuckers anytime. This money is ours! Ours! We worked hard for that damn championship!*

A knock on the door interrupted Maze's rant. And he knew exactly who it was.

"Chance," Maze said as he opened the door, "Come in."

"What happened this time?" Chance asked.

"Why do you assume the worst every time we talk?"

"Because that's the only time you call. Get to the point Seager."

"Ok. I need dirt on Orcon."

"Your boss? I thought y'all were cool."

"We were. Not now. I need to know about any shit that can fuck up his mayor campaign."

"When do you need it?"

"As soon as possible. Sooner than possible."

"I'll see what I can do." Chance said as he got up and shook Maze's hand.

"Appreciate the help, sir." Maze responded. He walked Chance out and closed the door.

We earned that money, he told himself.

CHAPTER 10

Calia caught herself staring at the poster behind Drame as he was giving his meeting report. It was a picture of a Leopard running past time, people, and even other animals toward victory. The setting looked like an African Savannah sunset. She thought it was cool that they didn't just have basketball all over the place. *Why can't I be running with you*, she asked the leopard to herself.

"Cal? Calia?!" Drame shouted. Calia readjusted herself in her seat.

"What? Oh! My bad. What...What did you need?" She asked.

"I said...do we have an update on the analysis for the Leopards website?"

"Oh...yeah...So... the new numbers can be added within 24 hours of games as long as everything is working correctly. It makes our stats the fastest in the NBA."

"Wow. That does sound fast." A deep voice from behind Calia answered. She turned around to see

Orcon enter the conference room. *Damn! He's finer up close,* Calia said to herself. But she tried her best to hide her big eyes when he came in and sat right next to her.

"Mr. Jessley! What are you doing here?" Drame asked.

"My apologies for interrupting. I just wanted to drop in and listen. I've been attempting to see all the departments just because." Orcon answered.

"This is truly a pleasure. We're not used to seeing you around these parts." Drame answered.

"Around a conference room?" Orcon asked with a smirk.

"Touché'. Well, might as well introduce you to everyone." Drame introduced all the team members. Orcon waved or nodded his head.

"And this is Calia LaCaze. She's been in the stats game probably longer than anyone at this table."

Orcon reached out his hand to meet Calia's. "Nice to meet you, OG Stats." Orcon said.

Calia chuckled. "I like that name. May have to get it tattooed on me."

"Guys...I know you have been working here for a minute, but I wanted to say thank you. We really appreciate everything you guys do to make sure that people know the numerical power each of our players have. It really is an important part of how the Leopards are able to be successful." Everyone smiled in agreement with Orcon. "Drame...you have the floor. My apologies."

"Thank you, Mr. Jessley. Next on the ag---"

"This is bullshit, Drame!" Colton Reese burst through the doors of the meeting. Calia put her head down and shook it.

"Mr. Reese. What is the problem?" Drame asked.

"I looked at my stats from the last game. Calia did not do my points right!" Calia raised her head and cocked it to the side. Her face was livid. Her fist was on the arm of the chair...waiting.

"Ok, Mr. Reese," Drame started, "How many points did you score, sir?"

"26! She gave me 20! I know she tripping because Dalion wasn't even in the game that long and he got six points!" Colton explained.

"So...let me make sure I have this correct. You interrupted our meeting over six points?" Drame asked.

"Fuck yeah! That shit matters to me! I want my fuckin' points!" Colton screamed at Calia. Calia looked at Drame in the eyes.

"Nobody give a fuck about you and yo' weak ass game!" Drame shouted at Colton.

"The fuck you just said to me?"

"You heard what I said!" Drame and Colton were face to face with steam coming off their faces.

"Guys...let's just try--" Orcon was cut off by Colton punching Drame in the face. Drame stumbled but came back and tackled Colton onto the ground. He started swinging fists left and right across Colton's face. Colton tried to kick him, but Drame was too fast with his punches.

"Don't... ever... talk... about... my... team!" Drame said in between punches. Orcon jumped over the table and pulled Drame off Colton and dragged him out the conference room while he was screaming "Fuck you! Whack ass Anthony Davis lookalike!" The others tended to Colton and tried to get a pulse and call an ambulance.

"Y'all...where's Calia?" Someone asked. They looked to find her on the floor next to her chair passed out.

CHAPTER 11

Beep......Beep......Beep......

Calia slowly opened her eyes to see a tile that said "Call. Don't fall." It had a picture of a person falling out of a bed. *Where the...hell am I?* She asked herself. She felt something stringy on her arm. She lifted it to see an IV poking out the top of her left hand. She followed the tube up to the source of the beeping noise: a heart monitor. *How the hell did I get here?* She wondered to herself. God, please do not let anyone be... "Ouch!" She screamed. A sharp pain radiated from the right side of her head. She looked for the NURSE button and squeezed it as hard as she could.

"How may I help you?" The Nurse asked.

"Orange...juice." She said as loud as a whisper.

"Say that again ma'am?" The Nurse asked.

"Orange...Orange..." Calia dropped the call button.

"Hold on. Someone will be there in a moment." The nurse replied. Calia closed her eyes and squeezed them tightly as another surge of pain came from her head.

"Ma'am...you needed somethin'?" The nurse asked.

"Orange....Orange....juice." Calia struggled to say.

"Orange juice?" The nurse asked. Calia nodded slightly. "Ok. We'll get you some orange juice."

"AAAAHHHHHHH!" Calia screamed before passing out.

* * *

"Sir? Mr. Reese just got out of surgery. Everything went well. Mr. Jones just suffered knuckle injuries, and Ms. LaCaze just woke up."

"Thank you, Tress." Orcon hung up the phone and sat back in his chair. He was glad everyone was ok, but it just didn't make sense. Drame has never been a violent type, and he's dealt with players like Colton before. What would make him get upset now? And why did Calia pass out from them fighting? *Something isn't right,* Orcon thought. He continued reviewing reports until his phone dinged to inform him of a text message. He slid up on his phone to reveal a link. *LEOPARDS Basketball NEW CEO the Son of a Drug Kingpin* Orcon's eyes widened. "Tress!" He screamed. "Get Taylor in here! NOW!"

* * *

"Thanks Pig. I owe you." Taylor said, hanging up the phone. "So... someone leaked the information to the *Dallas Morning News.* They tried tracing the source of the email, but it can't be traced. I'm sorry Orcon."

"So what's the next step?" He asked quietly.

"Well...you have 24 hours. You are going to have to either deny or admit. I can hold them off for that long, but after that something has to be said."

"Just 24 hours?"

"Yep."

"Shit. Ok." Orcon picked up his phone and keys. "I'll be back in 24 hours."

Chapter 12

So we will probably shiplap this entire wall and knock down the other in order to create the open concept that you want.

Open concept...Open thought...Oooh... open drive thru at 3 AM on a Saturday...Sonic...Sonic needs to be open at 3 AM...Their...Their Reese's blast is life... Wait... Am I on life support... Am I alive...

"Calia!" Denais jumped and moved to her bedside.

"How...How long was I out?"

"I've been here since this morning. When I came in, the nurses said you've been sleeping since yesterday. How you feeling?"

"Stiff," she tried to sit up, but her body did not cooperate. "Did anyone die?"

"Good question. I haven't heard anything yet. But your boss called to check on you. A Mr. Jessley?"

"Oh. That boss. Crap."

"What's wrong?"

"He was there. When it happened." Calia clicked the help button.

"Yes, how may I help you?" The nurse answered.

"Ask for orange juice." Denais ordered orange juice while Calia tried to gather her thoughts. *Are they dead? Did I kill someone? I knew it. I knew this would happen.*

"Good to see you awake, Ms. LaCaze." Calia turned to see a tall, chocolate skin black male with a white coat that accented his skin tone beautifully.

"Glad to be awake." She responded.

"I'm Dr. Awake. How are you feeling?"

"Stiff." She answered.

"That can happen after sleeping for about 3 days." His African accent flowed so easily when speaking.

"Three days?" Calia reached out for Denais' hand.

"Yeah...you've been in and out of consciousness. Your temperature has also fluctuated as well so we tried to keep you hydrated as much as we could."

"Am I ok?"

"Well...that depends on your definition...of ok. Your initial CAT scans show a pocket of mass pushing against the Amygdala. It's really small, but it would explain why you would be out for so long. Your body was trying to find a way to move it out of its place. Since it didn't move much, you slept longer. And yes, it is still there."

"Well can it be removed?" Calia asked.

"Not exactly. It has to be...exercised." Dr. Awake responded.

"Exercised? Like jumping jacks and push-ups?" Denais asked.

"Not quite. The Amygdala is a part of your limbic system. This system controls your emotions. This can make you feel extremes when you are happy or sad. It's... kinda like if Bipolar Disorder was on caffeine and alcohol at the same time. You feel heavy extremes to the point where your brain can shut down and operate automatically without your consent. Your brain goes into auto-pilot temporarily, and it makes you do things depending on the emotion you are currently feeling to others."

"So... I can control people's minds?" Calia asked. *Please say no. Please say no. Please say no.*

"Possibly. It only happens to .8% of people in the world, and everyone has a different reaction to it. The one common factor is passing out for long periods of time and the craving for orange juice after waking up."
"What do I do now?" Calia asked.

"I do not have a specific answer to that. But, if I'm honest, my sister, you need to find a way to control this before it is the death of you."

Chapter 13

Orcon wondered where the Burgundy Expedition in front of him was going. He could see loads of suitcases in the back, and he wished he was with them. With...a family. Not... alone. The idea of having witnesses to your triumphs and failures is taken for granted when drive and determination have control. It isn't for no reason. It is a defense mechanism. A defense mechanism that Orcon has not been able to turn off for over 30 years for fear of being caught off guard. It didn't help. It didn't help because front page news doesn't care about your past or your vulnerability. Orcon could reach and exceed bottom lines in business. He never wanted to be the bottom line for media embarrassment. He knew his dad was a great person who had to do not so great things in order to put food on the table and clothes on their back. He knew it was the best he could do within the means he had. The world wouldn't see it that way. They would see it as another black man turning to selling drugs and becoming a typical stereotype. That wasn't his dad. That wasn't the legacy he wanted people to associate him with. But now that it is out there, what could he do?

Things started to look familiar as he drove past the Burger King that signaled you were in Poedee, Texas. No amount of time could make him forget how to get to Jonas' house. Make a left at the Dairy Queen, pass Poedee High, and turn left where the tiger growls stiffly. The color of the house had changed, but the porch didn't. He stepped out of his car and made his way up to the house to ring the hummingbird doorbell.

"Who is it?"

"It's...It's Magic, Ms. Merry." The door slowly opened to reveal long silver hair crowning a caramel skin face. The bags under her eyes were a little deeper, but the ruby red lipstick with a long flowery dress and slippers revealed Ms. Merry, her best friend's mom.

"Magic? Baby, what you doin' here? Come in. Come in." He bent his head and stepped inside her home. The air conditioner made most of the silent noise in the living room that combined with the bidding of contestants on the *Price is Right.* He hugged her for a while. It had been a while since he felt such a sincere embrace from anyone.

"How are you?" He asked.

"Makin' it slowly but surely. It's been a minute since you've been here."

"Yeah...I know. You doin' ok?"

"As good as I can be. In between *Family Feud* and *Price Is Right* I haven't died yet." Her lighthearted chuckle made Orcon feel warm inside.

"Glad to hear that. Have you heard about Royalty

in the news?"

"No, I haven't. You know I don't watch that foolishness. I like my sanity."

"Oh yeah...I forgot. Someone leaked out to the news about my past. I... I don't know how to feel or what to do or...I'm just...lost."

"Well why? You knew who Royalty was."

"Yeah but...I'm trying to become Mayor of Dallas. How's the next Mayor look coming from someone who was a drug dealer?!"

"Bring yo' damn voice down! You know better."

"My apologies. I just...I know my dad was a good person with bad decisions to make. But how do I make others see that?"

"By being the man he wanted you to be. Look...you can't control your past or how it came to be a part of your life. You can only control what you do with it. You can run away from it. Or you can embrace it. Either way, it is a part of you."

"You're right. I know you right. And he would want me to push...by any means necessary."

"Exactly. I can't tell you how to deal with whatever people are saying. I can tell you that you ultimately have to decide how to handle your truth your way."

"Yes ma'am."

"Well... now that that's settled...let's guess how much this microwave cost."

Orcon smiled. "$1.00."

The Price Is Right turned into *The Young and The Restless* and memories of Magic and Jonas climbing trees and swimming in small pools. The sky started to turn orange outside Ms. Merry's screen door.

"Well...I better be headed back. Thank you, Ms. Merry. I...I really...needed this."

"Anytime baby. I'm glad you stopped by." They hugged and Orcon got into his car. He wanted to head home, but he felt like there was one more place he needed to visit. He passed through three stops signs and turned left. Glimpses of the sun were still kissing the granite tombstones as he walked through the grass to where his dad was buried.

Royalty Calhoune.
1968-1995.
Father, Son, Friend.

"Sup homie?" Orcon said to the grave then chuckled.

"I know you. You did what you had to do. By any means necessary. I'm really grateful for that. And...I don't feel bad about your choice. I just know how the rest of the world works. They are not as understanding. Still, you did it. And I can't change that. And you always taught me that a way is always possible if you want it bad enough. I want this mayor title. I can help Dallas be better than great. And I will. I promise I will." Orcon bent down and ran his fingers along his dad's name. He kissed the letters and left. He started his car. As he was turning back onto Plaintive Street, he called Taylor.

"Taylor. I got an idea."

CHAPTER 14

Well damn. He cute and his dad's a drug dealer? Calia said to herself. She watched Orcon's video on Instagram where he confirmed the allegation about his dad being a drug dealer.

"My past is my past. My dad was still a great person who chose to care for me when my mother wanted to be "free". While I don't condone his behavior, I will never forget how much he taught me or helped me to become a man. Whether you choose to vote for me or not is your choice, and I will respect it. But know...please know...my heart is for Dallas...by any means necessary."

Calia double tapped the video to like it. It was good to know she worked under someone who had flaws and was ok with them. She put her phone down and got up to head to the mailroom. She bumped into someone while she was looking at something on her shirt.

"Oh. My bad...Mr. Jessley."

"Hey Calia. Wow...you back to work already?"

"I figured two weeks was enough time to recover. And with Drame still recovering I knew people would need help. How are you?"

"I'm good. I should be asking you that question."

"I'm getting there. Work helps."

"Would you mind coming to my office?"

"Uh...sure. Like...right now?"

"Yeah...Yeah. Give me about 5 minutes to check something, and I'll be there."

"Ok." Calia headed back to her office, grabbed her phone, and headed to the elevator. As she pressed the button to the 12th floor, her mind started racing. She knew he had questions about her passing out when she did, and she was not ready to answer them.

"Um...Mr. Jessley wanted me to come to his office?" Calia told his secretary.

"Yep. He just told me. You can go in, Ms. LaCaze." Calia walked into the two big black doors with silver handles in the shape of leopards. The Margaret Hunt Hill Bridge welcomed her into the office. His windows held a beautiful view of the bridge above his chestnut desk.

"It's beautiful, huh?" Orcon asked. Calia jumped.

"The hell?! Jeez! You scared me! But yes, it is beautiful."

"Take a seat. How are you really feeling?"

"I'm ok."

"Did the doctors figure out why you passed out?"

"Not at this time," Calia lied. "But I'm probably going to go in for more tests soon."

"Does that happen often? The passing out?"

"Not really." Calia hoped her lies were convincing.

"What about the player stuff? Does that--"

"Orcon! What the hell?!" Orcon's doors bust wide open as Jordan makes his way into the office.

"Mr. McAfee. What is going on?" Orcon answered.

"I'm sorry, Mr. Jessley. I tried to tell him you were busy." Tress said.

"It's ok, Tress. Apparently what Mr. McAfee wanted couldn't wait." Orcon responded.

"Uh...do I need to come back later?" Calia asked.

"No...No...You are fine. You were invited," Orcon turned to Jordan. "What can I help you with, sir?"

"How in the hell are you going to trade my best player without talking to me?" Jordan screamed.

"Are you referring to Mr. Reese?" Orcon asked calmly.

"Who the hell else would I be referring to? Of course Reese!"

"Mr. Reese would be nothing for us after he would return from the hospital. I'm not spending time or money on someone who will not help cultivate wins in the Leopards organization."

"But you don't know that! You don't know what he could do for us! You could have waited! Even talked to me!"

"I could have, but I didn't. My decision is final, Mr. McAfee. And if you do not want this to be your last day, I suggest you leave my office, sir."

"Nigga, are you threatening to fire me?" Jordan shouted. Orcon was prepared to respond calmly, but something in his mind started burning. He started seeing red. Blood red. Jordan's words kept reverberating in his mind. It kept getting louder and pounding against his left and right temple. Rage took over.

"WHO THE FUCK YOU CALLIN' A NIGGA?!" Orcon shouted. Orcon lunged at Jordan and threw him to the floor. A cluster of fists pummeled into Jordan's face. Orcon saw blood, but he couldn't stop. Joy rose up from seeing Jordan's lips bust and his eyes turn purple and blue.

"Mr. Jessley? Mr. Jessley! Orcon! Stop! Stop!" Tress screamed running into the office. "Oh my God!" She screamed, calling 911 on her cell phone.

CHAPTER 15

A left temple pounding woke Calia up, but her eyes were still closed. She couldn't move, but she knew she was not home or anywhere she normally would be. She did feel carpet, and that felt comfortable.

"Calia? Ms. LaCaze?" She knew that voice. It sounded like a gentleman in his 40s.

"Yeah?" She answered.

"This is Mr. Jessley. Orcon." Bits and pieces started to slowly come back to her. Office. *Check in. Jordan. Nigga. Punches. Did I? Orcon? Fuck! Wait...why am I not in the hospital?*

"What happened?" Calia asked.

"You passed out. Again. Tress called 911 to save you and me...and hopefully Jordan."

No! Calia thought to herself. "What happened... to...to Jordan?"

"I don't know. He's on his way to the hospital with Tress. Are you ok?"

"Do you have orange juice?" Orcon went to the

back of his desk and grabbed orange juice from the refrigerator. Calia opened and started to gulp. Her eyes slowly opened to see Orcon sitting beside her with his hands bandaged.

"Oh my God. Are you ok?" She said holding her head.

"Didn't I just ask you that?"

"Oh. I'm better now. Still hurts but not as much."

"Ok. Can we talk about this pattern you have?"

"What pattern?" Calia asked innocently.

"A person's mad? Fighting happens? You pass out?"

"Well that was just a coincid--"

"Two times in a row is not coincidence." Orcon's cell phone started ringing.

"Tress? Hey. How is he? ...Oh. Ok. Call Lance and tell him to meet you at the hospital. Nobody leaves until Lance is there." Orcon hung up, put the phone down, and looked at his hands.

"What happened?" Calia asked, sliding into a chair.

"He's dead. Jordan is dead. I killed Jordan!" Orcon explained. Calia's migraine started to quietly throb.

"I... Mr. Jess... I'm sorry..." She burst into tears. Orcon leaned on his desk and lowered his head.

"This isn't coincidence, Calia. You're not telling me something." Orcon said quietly.

"I didn't mean...I...I can't..." She continued quietly sobbing.

"Calia. Stop. Breathe. Explain." He said sternly.

"It's my fault. When...when I get angry, I can't speak. I don't know how to express myself. So...so my mind...it makes people angry...it makes people...do bad things. I... I'm really sorry..."

"So... you can control people's minds?"

Calia nodded her head in agreement while sniffling.

"Why do you pass out?"

"I don't know how to control it. So...my body passes out. I'm really sorry. I didn't mean to..." Orcon walked over to Calia and kneeled down in front of her with a tissue.

"It's ok. It's ok. Don't worry. I'm going to take care of this. But you cannot speak about what happened in this office, ok?"

She sniffled. "Yes sir."

Chapter 16

Maze exited off of Royal Lane from Interstate 35. He turned left and drove for 2 miles. After seeing trees for most of the street, it was new to see a huge rusted barn on the right side of the street. He turned onto the gravel road and parked next to the huge black F350 sitting on 36-inch rims. "You have arrived." GPS said with a happy voice. Maze got out of the car and headed into the barn.

"Maze! What it do, homie?" Chance asked. They dapped each other up.

"I don't know man. He still wanna run." Maze responded.

"Seriously? I thought he would wanna to keep the 'goody two shoes' image."

"Me too. I got to get rid of this dude. He's screwing up my plans and my money."

"How much do you really want to get rid of him?"

"What do you mean?"

"Well...if he no longer exists...it ain't like he can

cause you that many issues."

"You mean like gone?"

Chance smiled then took a bit of his apple. Maze's eyes widened.

"No. I...I can't do that. I just don't need him playing with my money and what I earned!"

"Wow," Chance started, "You done with your tantrum?"

"You really are an asshole." Maze retorted.

"I know. But I'm consistent though. All I'm saying is that if you really want this dude out of your affairs, you have to eliminate the problem. Let me know when you ready to do that. I got actual work to do." Chance got up and left. Maze sat at the table with his back against the chair and his hand resting on his chin.

Eliminate the problem, Maze thought to himself.

CHAPTER 17

Calia fumbled with the keys getting into her dad's house. Her head was still throbbing all the way from the Leopards' office, and her boss' face kept replaying when he told her to not say anything about what happened to Jordan. She found the right key, opened the door, keyed in the alarm code, and closed the door. She sat on the bottom step of the stairs to stop the throb and think. She had time before her dad came home from work to find Blaine. She knew there had to be something in the house that could tell her where her grandfather was located.

She stood up from the step and headed to her dad's room. She searched his nightstand: Nothing. Closet and bathroom? Nothing. Chest of Drawers? Nothing. She left his room and moved to the guest room across from the living room. There was nothing in the drawers. She opened the closet. All of her old band uniforms were neatly hanging up below a shelf. She started to see some very familiar hats and shoes. They looked like something her mom would probably wear. She moved the shoes and hat to reveal a crimson box that was supposed to look like a treasure chest. She took the box down and sat it on the bed. When she opened it, she immediately smiled. It was a picture of her mother, Rachel. She was sitting on a sofa in a hotel room with her hands out and a huge smile on her face. Calia was sitting next to her giving her the Why-is-this-my-mom? look. The edge on Calia's pain went away as she started to remember Rachel and the warmth of her hugs. She kept digging to see Rachel in a graduation uniform with an older gentleman that looked like her dad. *That's Blaine. Talk about strong genes. Wow,* Calia thought. The picture was inside an envelope with an address in the top left corner.

Blaine LaCaze
611 Mansfield Avenue
Cancel, Louisiana 76502

Calia exhaled. The light at the end of the tunnel was here.

CHAPTER 18

"I... This is still crazy to me. He was in the best picture of health." Dane shook his head.

"This is all...crazy...to all of us. But Jordan was a great coach. Our time in this room needs to be spent making sure that our team now is all that he would want it to be. Thanks everyone. That's all for today." Orcon stated. Everyone started to file out of the conference room. Orcon sat in his chair staring out the picturesque window trying to figure out how to create a eulogy befitting Jordan's legacy and life while seeing invisible blood on his hands every day he went into his office. But he remembered what his dad used to say when he had to kill someone over his money, "Sometimes, death leads to a better life."

* * *

"So, we've been able to take care of everything for Jordan's funeral. The family was happy with your contribution to the expenses." Lance explained to Orcon.

"Good. Any more loose ends?" Orcon asked.

"The only I can think of is Calia. Have you talked to her?"

"No. She doesn't answer her phone. I really need to check on her too."

"About what she saw?"

"Not really. She has...a health issue that makes her pass out."

"Oh. Could we use that as a deflector to make sure to get people's minds off Jordan?"

"I don't think so. It only happens when she gets mad."

"Wait...what?" Lance stopped drinking his sweet tea. "What do you mean?"

"Well...she has this thing she does when she's angry. She can...kind of...control people's minds."

"Seriously?"

"Yeah yeah.... saw her do it twice. It was crazy. That's how I lost it. You know I don't care about people screaming at me. I really don't even remember touching him."

"So why are you protecting her? You could have just blamed her for this!"

"Lance, I did the act. She just controlled me, and she couldn't even control herself. That's not my style."

"I get that's not your style, but we are trying to win an election! Side tracking with this Jordan shit is making it harder for you to win."

"I know. And that's on me. But I can't do that to her. "Orcon said, taking another bite.

"Ok. Well...can she at least help?" Lance asked.

"The hell you mean?"

"So, she can make people mad and fight right? If we could get her to do that to some of the people in Campbell's camp...then..."

Orcon gave Lance a solid look. "Not my style, Lance."

"But you are always the one saying, 'By any means necessary'! If you want to win, sometimes this is how the game is played."

Orcon shook his head. "No, Lance."

"Look. You want to do better for Dallas, right? This is how you can do it. Let her do that dirty work. You already scratched her back. Let her scratch yours." Orcon contemplated Lance's words. His campaign wasn't doing as good as he wanted to. And after the information with his dad being a drug dealer came out, he was furious that someone would stoop that low just to keep their job. Once he had the Mayor position, he could change back and let go of the underhanded stuff he did just to get the position. Calia owed him. This was the least she could do. By any means necessary. Any. Means.

"Ok," Orcon started, "I'll find her."

CHAPTER 19

You've been acting kinda strange on me lately
Is there something on your mind?

I seem to get the feeling every time I'm near ya
That I'm running out of time...

D Train blasted through the surround sound speakers in Denais' condo. *Great song,* Calia thought, *but my head is killing me!*

"Uh...D... can we turn it down please? Trying to think here."

"Oops. You know how I feel about D Train!" She responded dancing around the dining room table.

"How can you dance around like this? I just killed someone!"

"Correction: Your boss killed someone. You just witnessed it." Denais kept dancing.

"Let's be real right now." Calia retorted. Denais stopped dancing and sat next to Calia on the sofa. Calia was scared to go home. She was scared to be anywhere. She knew this would happen, but why did it have to happen with her boss?! Of all people?! She wanted to think, but she was angry. Angry at her dad's side of the family. Angry that she couldn't control her emotions. Angry that she took someone's life.

"Yes ma'am. Have you heard from your boss since then?"

"No. I came here right after I left work. He told me he would take care of it. But what about the secretary? What about my job? I--"

"Calia Prise. Breathe." Denais said.

"I... I didn't mean to...D..." Tears filled Calia's eyes. Denais sat down and hugged her.

"I know it wasn't your fault, hun. But you can't do anything about it now. Except get help. Have you found your grandfather yet?"

"Yes," Calia replied in between sniffles. "He lives in Cancer."

"Then go see him. I'm sure your boss won't mind you taking off for a while." A notification ring interrupts Denais. Calia picks up her phone. Her mouth drops.

"What happened?" Denais asked.

"They just released that Jordan died. They said he died of natural causes."

"Wow. What kind of Olivia Pope fixin' they have going on?" Denais asked.

"I don't know, but I can't stay here to be a part of it."

"Then here. Take my car, some clothes, and money. Leave your phone here and get one of those prepaid phones. Go to Cancel. Just let me know when you make it."

Calia gave Denais a hug. "Thank you, D. Thank you."

CHAPTER 20

L-A-C-A-Z-E, C-A-L-I-A.

Orcon typed her name into the Leopards' Employee database. A profile popped her with her picture and personal information. He found her phone number to call her.

Hi. You have reached 469-555-1289. I'm either asleep, busy, or I just don't know your number. Leave a message, and I will get back to you.

Orcon hung up before the beep for the voicemail. He moved to her emergency contact, Denais.

"Hello?"

"Hello. May I speak to Denais Dingus?"

"This is she. May I ask who is calling?"

"This is Orcon Jessley. I work with Calia. She has your name listed as her emergency contact."

"Uh...well Hello. How can I help you?"

"I was wondering if you have seen or talked to Calia? I tried calling her phone, but it went straight to voicemail."

"Not as of today. But if I do talk to her, I will let her know."

"I would sincerely appreciate that. Thank you." Orcon hung up the phone. Damn, he said to himself. How else am I going to find this girl? He thought for a few moments until he had an idea. He dialed Maze's number.

"Hey O. You good?" Maze answered.

"Yeah...yeah. Just seeing if you still talk to... uh... Chance. Chance Piston."

"Chance? What do you want with him?"

"I need him to find someone for me. Someone who does not want to be found."

"That is his specialty. Who are you looking for?"

"Calia. Calia LaCaze."

"The statistician? What do you need with her?"

"Something for the campaign."

"Oh. You still running? Even with that stuff about your dad coming out?"

"It's going to take a lot more than the truth to stop me from helping Dallas. That's why I need Calia. I think she can help me."

"Oh. Ok. Let me see if I can find Chance. If I do, I'll let you know."

"Appreciate it Brother. Let me go handle some other stuff. I'll holler at you later."

"Watch dog?"

"Bow Wow. " Orcon hung up and sat back in the chair. *We got this Dad*, he said to himself.

CHAPTER 21

Chanson Papillon
We were very young
Just like butterflies
Like hot butterflies...

Chaka Khan's voice pierced every inch of Calia's ears to where she could not hear any wind or bugs smacking against her Nissan Altima as she traveled to Cancel. She was on the last end of her 8-hour trip through country, bumpy roads, and random billboards about a huge gas station with 32 restrooms. She didn't have time to make a playlist, but she did have time to stop by her house and grab some essentials before taking off. She grabbed the address for her grandfather, her huge case of CDs, and some other stuff she felt like she needed. She thought about calling her dad, but she decided against it. He didn't want to admit his dad was alive. Why would he care about her going down there?

She finally made it Exit 90: Cancel and Melodic. She took the exit and stopped at the first gas station she found to use the restroom. When she finished, she walked around and looked at the store. Pictures of alligators and fleur-de-lis covered brightly covered t-shirts hanging on the window. Random cups with weird sayings in French. "I don't give a Fais-Do-Do" caught her eye. She was heading towards it when a tempting aroma guided her to the hot plate line. She looked through the transparent window to see little balls that looked like fried chicken.

"Excuse me. What are those?" She asked.

"Fried Boudin Balls." The worker answered.

"Can I have one please?" The worker put two in a bag for her. She went back to the Fais-do-do mug, picked it up, and headed to the register.

"How you doin'?" The cashier asked.

"Good."

"Are you visiting? You don't look like Cancel folks."

"Yeah. Here to see my grandpa hopefully."

"Hopefully? He dead?"

"No... No. I never met him."

"What's his name?"

"Blaine."

"Blaine LaCaze?"

"Yeah. You know him?"

"Who don't? Really cool dude. Helped me a lot. Didn't know he had grandkids."

"He probably doesn't. My dad isn't a big fan of Cancel."

"Understandable... and not surprising. Most people are not, and we live here."

Calia grabbed her stuff. "Thanks. Have a good night."

"You too." She walked out the store and to her car. After putting her stuff away, she input the address into the car GPS and headed to see hopefully the one person that could help keep her from becoming a mass murderer. She did wonder how he would react. How long has it been since he talked to her dad? Did he have the same power? Could he control it? Why didn't his dad like talking to him? She had a lot of questions that needed answers and she hoped that she would have time to do it. The final left turn had her pulling into a one-story house that was multiple colors of brown and beige. The front yard had a garden full of zinnias and marigolds. There was a blue F150 parked out front that was almost as big as the house. She took a deep breath, got out of the car, and headed to the front door. She rang the doorbell.

She heard a TV commercial, so she knew someone was there. "Coming." He said. He opened the door. "Hello." He said in a strong but quiet voice. She froze. A little taller. His hair was grayer than anything. But she basically saw her dad staring back at her. "How can I help you?" He asked. Calia shook her head.

"Hi. My name is Calia."

"And?"

"Well...I'm...I'm Jayden's daughter."

"Jayden? My son? He still knows I exist?"

"Wait...what?"

"How did you find out about me? And where I live? I know he didn't tell you."

"Oh. You know your son."

"I'm sorry, baby. Come on in." Calia walked into the living room. The gray walls complemented the wooden floor and mahogany sofa set that sat against the left and right sides of the room. In the middle, a dark gray recliner sat with two light brown end tables. One table had his glass. The other table had a lamp along with the book *The Autobiography of Malcolm X* flipped upside down. Wheel of Fortune was playing on the flat screen TV hanging from the wall. She continued to scan the room to see pictures of men, women, boys, and girls with beautiful smiles and laughs on their faces. Calia sat on the left side sofa.

"So," Blaine asked, sitting in his recliner, "How the hell did you find me?"

"Well," Calia started, "I found an envelope with your address in a closet at the house. It was with pictures of Rachel."

"Really? I'm shocked he hasn't made that stuff disappear. How's your dad?"

"He's existing, I guess. We haven't talked for a minute."

"What's he doing now?"

"He works at a bank over the loan department."

"Well that sounds boring as hell." He responded. Calia chuckled at his statement.

"So what do you do?"

"I am... well was... the lead statistician for the Dallas Leopards. Not sure if I have my job now."

"What you mean?"

"Well... I made my boss kill someone."

"Made?"

"Yeah....with my...abilities?"

"Aw shit. Didn't your dad teach you how to control them?"

"No. That's why I'm here. I was hoping you could. My passing out is starting to get worse and I... I just want to be able to control myself and say how I feel without endangering myself or others."

Blaine nodded his head. "Fair enough. I don't know much I can do, but I will try. Tomorrow. After I finish watching *First 48*. In the meantime, unpack and relax. You can stay as long as you like."

Calia exhaled. Hopefully, the worst was over. She went and changed clothes. While she was in her room, she heard more than one voice coming from the living room. The voice sounded familiar but she couldn't quite remember where she heard it before. She grabbed her phone and went back to the living room. When she looked up, she saw the boy from the gas station.

"So you do know my grandpa." Calia said.

"Yeah. I told you Mr. Blaine is cool. I come over sometimes just to check on him after my shift." He answered.

"Oh. That's sweet. What's your name?" Calia asked.

"Novi. Novi Cartwright." Calia shook his head as she studied his physique. She knew he was tall, but outside of the gas station he was taller. His Caesar fade complimented his hazel eyes and round face. She liked his shirt that said "Sarcasm is My Natural Defense Against Stupidity", and his cargo pants did a good job of showcasing his muscular legs. *I would love to see him run*, she thought to herself.

"Uh...Calia?" Novi interrupted her concentration. She shook her head and smiled.

"My bad. Novi. Cool name." Calia replied.

"So is Calia." Novi responded. Blaine smirked.

"Well...since you all are here...why don't I cook?"

"OOO! You making Stuffed Cajun Bread?" Novi asked with a smile.

"Sure. Why not?" Blaine and Novi made their way to the kitchen. Calia looked at both of them. *I like him*, she said to herself.

CHAPTER 22

"It's hard to lead people who are like yourself: driven, determined, desiring a win. It takes a special personality that knows how and when to create the best chemistry and make magic. Jordan McAfee had that ability. He had the sense and knowledge of the game that made it possible to not just win but to teach life lessons. Never forget his abilities. Never forget his truth. Never forget the greatness that Jordan McAfee brought to the Leopards and to every single life he touched." Members of the congregation nodded and quietly murmured words of agreement. Orcon made it to his seat and exhaled. Orcon fought his conscience the entire time he was in Jordan's funeral. He was glad the family kept the coffin closed. That would have been too much.

As Jordan's body was put into the hearse, Orcon stood on the steps of St. Paul watching the family pour out of the church and head to their cars to go to the cemetery.

"You good boss?" Maze asked.

"I will be. You going to the gravesite?"

"Nah. Not for Jordan. I can't... I..."

"Yeah. I get it."

"So... what is it you wanted to talk to me about?" Maze asked.

"Did you get in touch with Chance Piston?" Orcon asked.

"You still want to talk to him?" Maze asked, disgusted.

"Yes. I need him to find someone that doesn't want to be found."

"Yeah...Chance is pretty good with that. I'll text you the number."

"Well can he meet us somewhere?"

"What do you mean 'us'?"

"Look...I know you may or may not be mad at me for my decision, but I know you will eventually understand the bigger picture. I'm going to need your help with this. You are one of the few people I can trust."

Maze paused. "Wow. Uh...ok. What do you need?"

CHAPTER 23

It makes sense why that pig was so happy in that commercial, Calia thought to herself. She put her head outside of her grandfather's F150 truck window and felt the country wind smack her face. She had to control her head to make sure she didn't get a concussion, but she didn't mind. She wasn't used to being able to put a window down and actually inhale air. She passed by fields with rows and rows of rice. Every once in a while, a house or farm with a cow pasture would pop up to accentuate the highway landscape.

"The hell you doing with your head out the window?" Blaine asked. Calia put her head back inside.

"Sorry. Couldn't resist. Where we goin'?" She asked.

"Somewhere you can't kill anyone." He smiled.

"So we have to go to the country to do that?"

"Yes. Less carnage. I used to take your dad out here to do the same."

"Why doesn't he like to talk about it?"
"Because of what he did."

"Did?"

"Yeah. Killed his best friend by accident when he was in high school. After that, he vowed not to use them again. I tried to explain to him that it wasn't his fault but...he couldn't get over what he did." Calia set back against the truck passenger seat. *Damn,* she thought to herself.

"Well...alright. That explains a lot."

"Yep. Made his best friend take his own life after they got into a really bad argument. He couldn't control it. By the time he came back from passing out, they pronounced his best friend dead."

"How can you be okay with this? This feels more like a curse than a blessing."

"Because of why we have it. But I can explain that later. Get out the truck." Blaine demanded.

Calia got out of the truck to see a huge white two-story house. It had the tallest columns holding up a triangular roof. Intricate little white baby angels danced across the top of each column. There were about 10 steps leading up to the porch with a glass two door entrance.

"Welcome to Passion Blood, baby." Blaine said.

"Passion Blood? Wait... is this a plantation?" Calia asked.

"Well, they are teaching y'all something in those

white schools."

"Why are we at a Plantation?" Calia asked.

"If you want to know about your powers, you have to start here."

"So I have to start at a place that oppressed slaves for hundreds of years? Really?"

"Yep. Oppression is not always a bad thing. Sometimes, it's a set for greatness. Come on. I'll show you around." Blaine led Calia past the "big house" to the yard where there were little shacks with withering wood. Some houses weren't bigger than a port-a-potty. Some were the size of a tool shed. An enormous green John Deere tractor smoothly drove across the fields behind the houses Calia looked around and started feeling shivers and tingles.

"So why did we come out here?" Calia asked, rubbing her arms.

"To connect." Blaine answered.

"Excuse me?"

"You heard me, chile. Connect. Your powers don't come from no crystals or witchcraft. They came from the hands and sweat of ancestors. Ancestors that toiled and turned these very fields."

"Like...slavery ancestors? The hell?"

"The hell is right. Our powers come from dealing with hell. When slave owners and masters would tear into the slaves flesh until they saw bone, the slave bodies would take the power from those lashings. The body would "cook" the power so-to-speak in our blood. The result of the cooking was our ability to do not-so-normal things. Some could control. Some could possess. Some could disappear. Some ran fast. Your abilities depended on your fear. The power would take your fear, cook it with the power, and provide you a supernatural way to conquer it."

"And this place is important because?" Calia asked.

"This is where your great-great-great grandparents received their powers. They were sold to Passion Blood from different plantations. According to my father, they stayed getting in trouble for something. Sometimes, they would get beat at the same time in front of people by the masters while holding hands. Then, after healing from the beating, they would come out here and practice their powers at night. They had plenty of chances to leave Passion Blood, but they chose to stay so others could leave. They helped others escape."

Calia looked at the houses. She moved toward the edge of the field where the tractor gathered rice. Her eyes started to see slaves. They were moving and humming as they heard the cracks of whips and high pitch voices of masters. No smiles were on their faces. Their bodies looked like two steps from death. But in their dark brown eyes, she saw hope. She saw power. She saw prominence. It's like they knew what was coming from their struggle and anguish. Calia closed her eyes. As the wind gently cuddled her face, energy surged from her feet, through her blood vessels, and all the way to the top of her head. Her eyes opened to tears falling but the biggest smile on her face.

"What...what were their names?"

"Uh...Jo Ann and Thomas." Blaine answered. Calia closed her eyes and whispered their names. "Jo Ann and Thomas. Thank you."

"Sometimes, knowing the pain makes the best progress. What you have is a painful gift. But it's a gift from pain. You have to learn when to let it work for you...not work you."

"How do I do that?" Calia asked.

"By challenging your fear. Right now, your fear is driving your life, and your powers are using that to do things without your permission. Stop letting fear drive and take control. Tell me something. When do you blackout?"

"Usually some type of anger or argument is about to happen."

"So...your fear is confrontin' stuff?"

"Well...yeah. I don't like seeing people mad or unhappy."

"Wow. That's sad." Blaine responded.

"What do you mean?" Calia asked with an attitude.

"You think things are always perfect or they have to be perfect. But imperfections are how you got your abilities. You gotta learn to be okay with problems. They happen sometimes. It don't mean things are bad. It just means trouble has to happen to get back to good."

"But why! Why do people have to fight? Why don't people listen and understand? What's wrong with wanting that?"

"Nothin' is wrong with wanting that. You just can't have it that way. Humans don't operate like that. Think about it: How great would the bible be if Adam and Eve didn't do anything stupid? Nobody would learn nothing! You gotta learn to respect conflict for what it is."

Calia felt her body nerves freeze. She felt her brain click and switch over to a place where she no longer had control.

"Then fuck this place! Nobody deserves to live if they can't do it my way!" She screamed.

Blaine stepped back. "Your way," He started calmly. "Ok. What's your way?"

Calia went silent. She was looking for someone. Someone to control. Someone to possess. Someone to express the rage erupting in every single inch of her body. She looked at her grandfather. She tried to control him. Nothing happened. He just stood there. Smile on his face. Sun making a halo around his head. She tried again. Nothing changed. Her body started to give in to losing what was left of strength.

"I said," Blaine started, "What is your way?"

"My way...my way is..." Calia fell to the ground.

CHAPTER 24

"Can you sign these Mr. Jessley?" Tress asked. Orcon laid his signature to the final two contracts to seal the deal on new members coming to the Leopards.

"Done. Send these over to Finances to make sure the numbers line up. Thank you." Orcon closed the tablet and Tress left the room. He sat in silence for a minute. A lot had happened over the course of two weeks, but his goal did not change. Mayor of Dallas. By any means necessary. He knew that with Calia's powers and his silver tongue no one stood a chance against him. He also knew that Calia wasn't stupid either. He needed to make sure she understood the good it could do with her on his squad. If only he could find her...

Orcon opened his drawer to find his burner phone. He dialed the one number in the phone.

"This is Chance." The voice answered.

"Hey. How are you doing?" Orcon asked.

"Really? You asking that? To me? Boy get the hell on. What do you want?" Chance asked annoyed.

"I was just checking to see if you found the package yet."

"She not in Dallas if that's what you asking. She's also not in her car or with any of her valuables. We checked her spot and we kept surveillance on her cousin's house. Nothing. We've been looking at her dad's house for a couple of days too. It's just him. You think he would know something?"

"Maybe. Any way you can find out?"

"I got ways. Meet me tonight at 11 to find out. I'll text the address."

"Will do." Orcon hung up the phone and placed it in his pocket. He picked up his work phone and called Maze.

"Maze," he started, "What you doin' at 11 tonight?"

* * *

"You have arrived." GPS said with a happy voice.

"The Red Barn." Maze said as they got out of the car.

"I'm assuming you know this place." Orcon said quietly.

"Yeah...a little too well." Maze replied.

They opened the door to hear slaps and punches. They turned and saw somebody tied to a chair with blood streaming down his face.

"I told you. I don't know where she is!" He

screamed.

“Come on Chance. Maybe he don’t know.” One of the other men said.

“What the hell?!” Orcon screamed.

“Mr. Jessley. How nice of you to join us!” Chance exclaimed.

“Chance! Who is this?” Orcon asked.

“Orcon Jessley: Meet Jayden LaCaze, Calia’s dad.” Chance announced.

“Mr. LaCaze. Nice to meet you. I apologize for this. We just want to know where Calia is if possible.” Orcon explained.

"I told y'all. I don't know where she is. She hasn't talked to me for weeks!"

Chance raised his fist to continue his interrogation, but Orcon stopped him. "Ok. So you don't know where she is. Do you know where she might be?" Orcon asked.

“I can’t...think of...anywhere.” Jayden answered in between breaths.

“Guess we need to move to more effective methods to get some answers.” Chance announced loudly.

“No,” Orcon interrupted, “We don’t. If Jayden doesn’t know, let him go.”

“Excuse me?” Chance asked.

“I said Let Him Go. I’ll find another way.” Orcon

restated. He started untying Jayden.

"I know this mother fucka didn't--" Chance started moving toward Orcon. Maze blocked them.

"Let him go. Just...let him go. We have other...plans." Maze said firmly but quietly. Chance backed off. Orcon helped Jayden up and headed towards the car. "You comin' Maze?"

"Uh...nah. I'm going to stay. I need to chop it up with Chance for a second anyway. Go ahead and take Jayden home. I'll catch up with you later." Maze answered.

Orcon reached his car and helped Jayden into the passenger side. Then, he got into the driver's side and pressed the START button for the ignition.

"I apologize again, Mr. LaCaze. This wasn't what was supposed to happen. I just wanted to find your daughter."

"Y'all sure as hell got hurtful ways of doing that. Go 635 North." Jayden responded.

"I asked Chance to find her, but I didn't ask for all this."

"Why do you want to talk to her?"

"To see if she will help with my campaign. I think she can help me win some young adult votes."

"Is she a people person like that?"

"She seems to get along with everyone well at work. Her boss thinks she's awesome."

"Oh. That's...that's good to know. Exit on Marsh Lane and make a left at the light."

"You and her don't talk?"

"Not often. We do better separately than together." Jayden responded quietly. Orcon nodded his head.

"Ah...Got it. Well maybe things will change. Keep straight?"

"Yeah. Make a left at the next street." Jayden answered. Orcon turned left on Rosemark Avenue.

"It's the second house on the left. Right here." Orcon pulled up in front of the house. He put the car in park and then took out a business card.

"Here's my personal phone number. If you have any hospital bills or..."

"Ahhhh.... I'll be fine. Not like I haven't been punched before. Thank you anyway. If I hear from Calia... wait... I think I know where she is. It's a far shot, but you can try it."

"Where?"

"Cancel. Louisiana. My hometown."

CHAPTER 25

Calia's eyes felt hot beams of sunlight beating the daylights out of her eyes. She wanted to open her eyes, but her eyelids were not having it. A rhythmic thumping played against her temples and slowly crept to the front of her head.

"Hmmm..." She moaned.

"Ah...Sleeping Beauty hath returned. Need some orange juice?" Blaine asked.

"MmmHmm..." Calia answered quietly. Blaine placed a cold jug in her hand. Calia sat up slowly, eyes closed, and chugged the orange juice until her headache slowly dissipated.

"You good?" Blaine asked.

"No...Did I...uh...try to..." Calia started.

"Yep. Ya' did. But you didn't know that your powers do not work on people who already have them."

"Ah...well alright. Good to know." Blaine picked Calia up from the ground. Her eyes were open now, and she could see the open field again.

"Ready to try again?"

"Yeah. Let's try this again." She said.

"So, when do you usually blackout?"

"When I'm angry or an argument is about to happen around me."

"Why?"

"I... I don't like seeing people unhappy."

"Because?"

"It means there is something wrong, and I cannot fix it."

"But that's not your job. You ain't on this earth to fix people or their problems. You gotta live your life like everyone else. Who is somebody you have been upset with lately?"

"My dad. Your son."

"So if you could talk to him, what would you tell him?"

"I didn't really understand why he wouldn't help me control my powers. I... I just wanted him to understand that I don't like making people fight or be confrontational. I know he's still angry about mom. I know he has a lot to think about. But it doesn't mean that I'm ok too without him. I just want him to understand that I want a better relationship. I want to be able to release my anger in a healthy way instead of destroying the lives of people I know and don't know. I can't control what happened in the past. I can control what happens in the future with his help."

"See what you did? You said what you meant and meant what you said. That's all it takes to control your powers. Speaking your truth. The reason that has been so hard for you is because you want to try to not ruffle any feathers or ripple the water. You can't do that, baby. You gotta say it. Get it out. I'm not saying you have to scream and act like a ghetto black woman. You do have to exercise your right to say what you feel even if it will hurt someone."

"But how do I practice that? How do I...you know...do that all the time?"

"Practice! You got any friends?"

"Denais, my cousin."

"Aw hell...she would be perfect. Practice with her. Ask her to take you through moments like that. But make sure she on the phone or somewhere where you can't see her. The first couple of times are gonna be rough but it will get better." Blaine wrapped his huge arm around Calia. "You gone be alright, girl. You just have to remember that your voice has power too."

Calia exhaled. *My voice has power,* she said to herself. She smiled as they went back to the truck.

"Grandpa? Do you know where my mom is buried?" Calia asked quietly.

"Yes. West Cancel Cemetery. Wanna visit?" Blaine asked.

"Yeah...I think I can now." Calia answered. They hopped in the truck and drove back into town. When they got to the cemetery, Calia took a deep breath.

"You good?" Blaine asked.

"Yeah...let's go." Calia said as she got out of the truck. They walked up to a low hanging tree to find a gravestone with a beautiful angel resting on the top

.

Rachel Dingus LaCaze
Sunrise: May 13, 1970
Sunset: August 16, 1999
Because God needed more angels...

Calia exhaled. She didn't realize she was holding her breath until she saw her mom's name engraved in granite. "Yeah...I was shocked your dad actually let her body come home. I thought after he left Cancel that he didn't want nothin' to do with anything. But... her family insisted...with they over religious asses."

"Yeah...Denais told me. Why were they like that?"

"It was Rachel's mom fault. She had bags on bags of skeletons in her closet. She thought marrying a pastor and changing her status would help the skeletons not see the light of day. For the most part, it did. Except with us. We can't afford to hold nothin' in especially with our gifts. Guess that's why Rachel and Jayden clicked. She wasn't like the rest of her family. We accepted her for who she was."

Calia's eyes started to water. "Wow." She said quietly. She only saw the mean side of her dad. She couldn't believe that he actually had a heart at one time in his life. "Can I have a minute alone with her, please?" Calia asked.

"Sure. I'll be in the truck." Calia folded her arms.

"Um...hi. I'm sure you know who I am. I just...wanted...well...I just...why are you not here? Well...I know why you are not here, but I don't understand why God would take someone so pretty and sweet and honest away from us. Away from me. I want it to make sense. But it doesn't. I'm sorry... I'm wasting your time with questions you cannot answer. I just want you to know I'm... I'm better. Grandpa helped. My voice is my power, and I want to use it instead of my fears. Thank you. Thank you for being what you could at the time with what you had. Thank you for choosing love. I... I hope you are proud of me. I hope that I'm doing what you can appreciate. I love you. Ok...Bye." Calia smiled as she tasted salty tears coming from her eyes.

CHAPTER 26

"You idiot! How did you miss that block?!"

Orcon walked into Cade's mansion to hear Janice, his widow, shouting. Sometimes, Orcon wondered who the bigger sports fan was. When Cade was alive, she and Cade would be in the suite, sitting next to each other, comparing stats of the different players. People also knew not to sit so close to Janice for fear of losing their eardrums. Orcon shook his head and smiled as he made his way towards the den.

"Hey Mama Bear." Orcon greeted.

"Hey ba--Shit! The hell you doin', Douglas?"

"Ah...the Bears making you mad yet again?"

"Of course. Their defensive line acts like they scared to touch someone! I'm sorry. Let me turn this off. How you doin', baby?"

"I'm tired."

"I would be too if I was trying to run a basketball team and be a mayor. You sure you not taking on too much?"

"You know I don't know the answer to that question."

"Ok, O. Keep playin'. Your heart will make the decision for you if you don't slow down. God took 7 days. It's ok for you to take your time to get what you want."

"I have to prove something, you know? Like I'm not better than my past. I can't help who my dad was."

"You right. You can't. And if you are trying to outrun your past, gone head and turn in your cleats. It's not gonna happen."

"Mama J..."

"Look...your past is not going anywhere. But if you don't stop trying to live above it, you gone be the one dead...not your past. And think about it. It's because of your past that you are here. You had people who toiled fields, sold drugs, stayed on their knees praying...just so you could be here. I'm not saying everything they did was right, but they did what they could with what they had."

"But I'm not them!"

"Who the hell you hollerin' at?"

Orcon took a deep breath. "I'm sorry Mama J... I just get tired of people telling me that my past is a part of me. Don't get me wrong...I know my dad did what he could, but that's why I strive to do better by any means necessary. I don't want to end up like he did."

Janice turned off the TV and stared Orcon directly in

the face. "If you keep going with that "by any means necessary" attitude, you gone end up in the same place as him."

"You know what? Ok. I'm glad you are alright. I love you. Talk to you later, Mama Bear." Orcon stood up, kissed Janice on the forehead, and walked out of the house shaking his head. He needed to be around someone who would understand his point of view.

"Google: Directions to Maze Seager's House". It was a Sunday afternoon, so the Dallas North Tollway was clear for him to make it to Maze's house in less than 20 minutes.

"Well this is unexpected. Sup homie?" Maze said as he opened the door.

"I wish these mother fuckers would understand!" Orcon said walking into Maze's house.

"Well damn. We coming out the gate strong, huh? You want a drink?"

"Yep." Maze walked over to his bar and poured him a double of Monkey Shoulder.

"Why can't everyone see that what I'm doing is the best for everyone?"

"What do you mean, O?"

"I went to talk to Mama Janice. She told me to slow down. That me trying to do everything is 'too much'. I know what I can and cannot do, Dammit!"

"Well...if you know you can do this...why worry about what people think?"

"I...well I...shit. Good point. I don't need them to get what I want. I know exactly what I'm doing."

"There you go. Now that we've solved the problem of your world peace, you found that girl yet?"

"No. But her dad gave me a possible place. It's this place called Cancel? In Louisiana? I'm going to go and see what I can do."

"All this for some campaign stuff? Really O?"

"This girl can control people, Maze. Control their minds. Control their emotions. Do you know how much I can do with that in the city of Dallas?!"

"Yeah," Maze started, "You could do a lot."

"Plus my dad said that if you want something you gotta get it...by...say it with me..."

"Any means necessary." They said together.

"Well...let's toast. To getting what we want when we want it." Maze raised his glass in the air.

"By any means necessary." Orcon replied.

CHAPTER 27

"Oh my God! This is amazing!" Calia gushed.

"You tellin' me your dad never cooked gumbo for you?" Blaine asked.

"No. Well if he did I don't remember. After Mom died, he didn't want any reminders of Louisiana I guess. He embraced Texas for better or worse. But this...this is amazing!"

"Well I'm glad you like it. And you can thank your grandma for this. That woman knew she could burn. Every time I cook I feel closer to her."

"What was she like?"

"Your daddy's defense mechanism comes from her. She never knew how to deal with conflict, but she knew how to cook. She also had the greatest smile. When she was with me, she was so relaxed and fun. She couldn't do that with her side of the family."

"I'm noticing a pattern. What is it with the black people in Cancel?"

"Small town mentality. Most of these people don't

know anything beyond Cancel. There are a few of us who can see beyond the city limits. Most of us who do leave. Those who stay, like me, don't mind those people. They leave me alone, and I leave them alone. Lemme go answer this phone." Blaine left the kitchen. Calia savored every single morsel of the chicken and sausage gumbo with cornbread. *What have I been missing?!* Calia asked herself.

"Your friend is on his way." Blaine said jokingly.

"What friends I got? I just got here last week!" Calia asked.

"Novi. You really think he's been by here every day for me? I barely see him once a week."

Calia smiled. "He just met me. What could he possibly want with me?"

"Well," Blaine started, "You are not a cousin. Second, you are different from most Cancel women. Plus, you are beautiful. I don't have no ugly grandkids!"

Calia giggled. "Wow. Those seem like some high standards. I'm surprised I made the cut. What do you think about Novi?"

"I'm proud of him. He could have ended up just like his sisters and brothers in jail. He chose a different path. I'm just around to make sure he stays on that separate path."

"Good to know. Thank you. I'll get the door."

"Novi! Good to see you. How are you?"

"Better. Your beautiful face helps. How are you?"

"In heaven with Grandpa's food!" Calia exclaimed as she took Novi's hand and guided him to the table where a bowl of steamy gumbo was waiting for him. Together they talked for over two hours about everything from the different eras of the MLK Park to Macon's Pizza changing their recipe but not their prices. Calia listened to their down-home southern voices and started to feel a little jealous. Their voices had a short drawl that lingered even after they finished cutting off the end of a word. Her Texas bred voice sounded so snooty compared to their voices.

"Can I ask a random question?" Calia asked.

"Sure. Shoot." Blaine answered.

"Why doesn't my dad's voice sound like yours?" Calia asked.

Blaine thought for a moment, then shrugged his shoulders. "Good question, baby. Could be that your dad worked hard to forget this place that he tried to sound like those Texans more than anything. When he was living here, his accent was worse than mine."
"I didn't think it was possible to even get rid of this voice." Novi added.

"It is. When you work hard enough, you can forget anything you like. The problem comes in when it don't forget you." Blaine stated.

"Yeah...that part." Calia agreed. Blaine yawned for the third time.

"Ok kiddos. I'm goin' to sleep. I'm old, and I got good food in my stomach. Calia, lock up when Novi leaves, please?"

"Will do. Goodnight, Grandpa." Calia said as Blaine walked out the room. She and Novi stayed in the kitchen eating orange sherbet in silence for a minute. Sometimes, he would look up. Sometimes, she would look up. When they looked up together, they immediately went back to their bowls full of semi-soupy sherbet. Novi finally broke the silence.

"Cancel hasn't made you tired, yet?" Novi asked.

Calia smiled. "Not yet. It's not as fast paced as Dallas, but I'm ok."

"Would you like to see more?"

"More of what? Y'all got more than one stoplight?" Calia joked.

"We do. But there are some other places you might enjoy. Unless Texas has made you scared."

Calia raised an eyebrow. "Really? Scared? Around here? Boy please."

"Ok. What about tomorrow? I'll take you on my personal tour of Cancel, Louisiana."

"Sure. What time?"

"8 PM?"

"Works for me."

"Cool. I'll see you tomorrow." Novi got up, washed

his bowl, and headed out of the door. Calia followed behind and locked it. She stood there for a minute and exhaled. Then, she went back to her bowl of Orange Sherbet with a vengeance.

* * *

As much as she enjoyed Cancel weather, Calia did not enjoy mosquitoes. She looked in the mirror at her mosquito-proof outfit: a light white off-the-shoulder long sleeve blouse complimented by light blue skinny jeans. White low top converse donned her feet along with multicolored earrings in the shape of Africa that said, "Africa is Love". *Damn, Grandpa really don't have ugly grandkids,* she said to herself.

"Calia! Novi's here!" Blaine shouted.

When she made it to the living room, Novi was dressed in all black like an expensive Sharpie. The LA hat complimented his face while the Black Lives Matter short sleeve tee rested comfortably on his chest.

"G-Nikes?" Calia started. "You went old school, huh?"

"Only the best for you." Novi answered.

"That's fair. Grandpa...we'll be back. I got my key."

"Novi...take care of my baby, yeah." Blaine stated.

"Yes sir. See you later." Novi answered. They got into Novi's Toyota Land Cruiser.

"So, Tour Guide, where to first?" Calia asked.

"Macon's Pizza. You are going to need nourishment

for this trip." Novi answered. They talked while iLL Camille spilled from the stereo speakers. The conversation continued into Macon's Pizza where they each had plate for plate of the buffet pizza. Then, they headed to the arcade room and played three rounds of air hockey...that Calia won. They left Macon's and headed to Sagittarius: a late-night music spot that you heard from a block away. They parked about a block away from the club and headed in to listen to a mixture of Jazz Fusion and Hip Hop. Novi watched as Calia's eyes lit up as she watched each musician have their own solo in the midst of freestyles and beats. In between different artists, they would talk about the differences between music styles of some of their favorite artists. They left the club holding hands on the way back to the car.

"That. Was. AMAZING!" Calia exclaimed.

"I'm glad you enjoyed it." Novi answered.

"So...where to next?"

"Honestly, there was one more place. But I don't feel like fighting mosquitoes tonight."

"I appreciate you for that. I can live without that too. What about your house?"

Novi gave Calia a confused look. "My house? I don't live like Mr. Blaine."

"I don't care." Calia said softly.

"Ok. My house it is." Novi started his Land Cruiser and headed home. He changed the music to D' Angelo's *Voodoo* album. They drove quietly with Calia's head on Novi's right shoulder. It had been a while since she felt safe with someone. She didn't have to pretend or compete. She liked that she could be herself...old school and all.

Novi pulled up to a two-story apartment building. They hopped out of the truck and headed to his apartment on the first floor. When he opened the door, the smell of lavender greeted Calia. His living room was simple but cool. He had a brown sectional that looked like a Care Bear's cousin. The walls were covered with African art and inspirational sayings.

"Wow. I didn't expect you to live like this." Calia stated.

"So, you thought I was going to have little weed stashes everywhere and pictures of me throwing up the middle finger with wads of cash to my ear?"

"Well, that was my second thought. Did you do these?"

"Nah. My friend, Delvis, did. Dude is amazing with a brush and paint. Did you want anything to drink?"

"Water? Please? I've had enough to drink." Calia sat down while Novi went to the kitchen. One of the quotes in his living room caught her attention: "One day, your silence will be the death of you. Kelita Johnson". *Ouch,* Calia thought to herself. *I feel convicted.*

"Seriously, your apartment looks awesome. Why the quotes?" Calia asked.

"They help me stay on track. I don't know if Mr.

Blaine told you, but my family is not exactly the most...nurturing." Blaine answered.

"What do you mean?"

"Dad died due to drugs. Mom wasn't the motherly person either. So, me and siblings had to fend for ourselves. I was the only one to not end up in jail."

"Wow. Where's your mom?"

"Somewhere in South Carolina. She decided to follow some dude up there. Haven't heard from her in 7 years or so."

"Hold up. You have kids and you don't even want to check on them?"

"I told you. Not the most motherly person."

"I can understand that. My dad changed after my mom died. I don't remember much from before 7 years old. I do remember one time when all of us opened presents on Christmas Eve because Mom had to work Christmas Day at the hospital. I gave her this macaroni picture frame I made in class. She hugged me so tight that day. My dad's smile almost looked like the Joker from Batman."

"See? Your dad is human. Technically."

"Exactly. Technically. How do you cope with not having parents?"

"I have other people in my life that fill that void: Mr. Blaine. Ms. Jackee'. They keep me from going completely insane. What about you?"

"My cousin Denais. She provides me sanity when the world says otherwise. But it also helps to have a job that deals with something you love."

"You love stats?"

"Yes, I do. I know Math is difficult for some, but I see things clearer in numbers. Everything just makes sense, you know? Like understanding the shooting average of players from the 3-point line is intriguing."

"Well...maybe all those Math classes in high school actually meant something."

"If you listened, they did."

"You are definitely different. I like it."

Calia moved to sit next to Novi. "You are too. I guess differences attract. "She said quietly. Novi leaned in and kissed Calia on the lips. Calia closed her eyes and smiled while kissing Novi. He pulled away.

"You ok?" He asked quietly.

"Yes...it's just been a while." Calia answered.

"Oh. So, I'm giving you a review of what kissing is?" Novi asked.

"In a way."

"Ok. Well, not much has changed. Except now men like to ask for consent before doing anything. It's not as sexy, but it keeps us out of jail. That's all you are missing. So, can I kiss you, again?"

Calia chuckled. "Yes. You can." They kissed and

held each other's faces. Calia experienced many different kisses before. Some sloppy. Some dry. Some confusing. She laid back on Novi's sectional and let her arms and hands discover other parts of Novi she wanted to explore since they first met in the gas station. His skin was soft. His body felt like mountains and valleys of peace.

"Can we take our clothes off and can we have sex? Just asking both to get them out of the way."

Calia laughed. "Yes and Yes. You are a fool." They continued to kiss and take turns removing different pieces of clothing. As much as she works on her body, Calia is always nervous when it comes to being naked in front of anyone. When they were fully naked, Novi paused.

"Wow." He said.

"What? What's wrong?" Calia said.

"You...you look amazing." Novi said quietly. Calia blushed and Novi kissed her blushed cheeks.

"Wait. I need to do something really quick. Can we go to my room?"

"Uh...Ok?" Calia replied. They left their clothing on the floor and went to Novi's bedroom. He guided here to the bed. "I'll be back." He went to his stereo, looked until he found a CD and put it in his CD player.

"Who still has a CD besides me? Answer: Novi does." Calia said. He pressed play, and Usher's *My Way* album started playing.

"Oh wow. This is a throwback." Calia stated.

"Yeah...Kinda always wanted to do it to this album." Novi answered, crawling under the covers.

"I'm glad I could fulfill a wish." Calia replied as they fell onto the bed and into each other's arms.

Chapter 28

Maze looked through his sunroof into the night sky. The green neon lights from the Downtown Omni Hotel were spinning and gyrating like James Brown on a stage. He thought it was a four-leaf clover, but it was nowhere near St. Patrick's Day. *UNT must have won something*, he thought. He closed his eyes. Images of Orcon speaking at the luncheon, the funeral, and the Red Barn played across his mind. *Why does he have to be so damn driven?* Maze thought. I can't keep doing this. *He has to go. Soon.* A knock on his passenger door interrupted his thoughts.

"Still ducking off in cars I see? Jealous ex or bookie you owe?" Chance asked.

"Depends on which day you ask me." Maze answered.

"So what's this idea of yours?"

"You know the girl Orcon is looking for? Calia? This chick can control people!"

"Control people? Like take over their mind?"

“Yep. But she only makes people angry and wanna fight. That’s why Orcon wants her so badly. To help with his campaign.”

“Smart move if I’m honest. But how’s that gone keep us from doing the deed? We don’t know where she at.”

“He told me she’s in Cancel, Louisiana. We can go down there, hold her hostage, and make her kill Orcon!”

“But why would she wanna do that for you? She know you?”

“No. But I’m sure she won’t be happy to know that some money is gone and she’s not getting a raise. Plus, I have yet to find someone who liked being held hostage.”

“Well some of the strippers from Onyx don’t mind if-”

“Spare me your sex escapades, Chance. I’m good.”

“So what’s the next move, boss?” Chance asked.

“Pack your bags. We are going on a trip.” Maze answered.

CHAPTER 29

Blaine dug the hoe deeper into the soil. He's been pulling weeds and checking vegetables for 2 hours, but to him it felt like 30 minutes. "This soil is stubborn today, Della. Why you didn't you toil earlier this week?" He said out loud. Garden time was when him and Della had their best conversations even after her death 21 years ago. It was like she personally made sure that the tomatoes were the juiciest, the greens were the fluffiest, and the bell peppers shined like pure green gold. He heard a car ignition stop along with someone getting out of a vehicle, but he assumed it was for the Richards next door. They always had random people at their house. A knock on his front door stopped his conversation with Della. "Who the hell you got at my house this early Della?" Blaine went to the front door and opened it.

"Yes?" Blaine asked.

"Uh...Hello. Mr. LaCaze?"

"Yeah. Who are you?"

"I'm Orcon Jessley. I work with your granddaughter, Calia."

"Ok. And?"

"I wanted to see if I could talk to her about something."

"She ain't here, but she should be back soon. Come in." Blaine gestured. Orcon sat on the couch.

"What you want with Calia?" Blaine asked forcefully.

"I came to check on her, sir. Plus, I wanted to ask her to do something for me with my campaign. I'm running for mayor in Dallas."

"Oh really? Well congrats. But you couldn't tell her this on the phone or somethin'?"

"I tried to call her but she didn't answer. So your son, Jayden, told me she may be here."

"Jayden? Really? I'm shocked he still knows this place exists. But how will Calia help with your campaign?"

"Well...I found out that she has these...abilities. And I want to see if she will use them for me."

"Oh...so you know about her powers?"

"Yes sir. I...uh...know them very well."

"And you know it only happens when she angry? And she makes people hurt themselves? You wanna campaign based on hurting people?"

"I know it's not the best way to win, but it's what I have. And my dad always said that sometimes push got to shove."

Blaine sat back in his recliner. "Hmm. Push got to shove, huh?"

"Yes sir."

"So if you can't do the pushin' and shovin' yourself, why you runnin' for Mayor? Seems to me like you act like you confident and can do everything, but you scared. Runnin' scared. And if your campaign is gonna depend on a girl who got anger problems, you don't have a chance in hell when it's hot or cold."

Orcon took in a deep breath, and then he exhaled. "I can definitely see your viewpoint."

"I'm not gone stop you from asking her, but I hope you know what you are doing." Blaine answered rocking in his recliner. The key on the front door turned. Calia walked in and stopped midstep.

"Mr. Jessley? How...How did you..."

"Your dad. Your dad told me where he thought you were. Turns out he knows you more than you think."

"What are you doing here?" Calia asked.

"I came to check on you first. Are you ok?" Orcon asked.

"Yeah...yeah...I'm good."

"Good. Second, I wanted to ask you something."

"Novi? Let's go outside. I need some help with Della in the garden." Blaine said getting up.

"You and Della at it again? What she did wrong this time?" Novi asked as they left out the back-sliding doors of the kitchen. Calia turned her focus back to Orcon.

"So...what's your question?" Calia asked sitting down on the sofa.

"You have an incredible gift. Even with what you made me do to Jordan, I still see the potential in what could happen if you used your abilities effectively. So what about using them...for me? For my campaign?"

Calia squinted her eyes. "Your campaign?"

"Yes! You can help me to get rid of Campbell! You see how he's been treating Dallas! I could do so much more for the D. Better jobs! More funding for education and schools. More businesses and growth. I'm telling you...Dallas deserves me. I know your powers only work when you are angry, but that's ok. We...we can find a way to make you... "

Orcon continued talking, but Calia's mind was already gone. She felt her body go numb, and she did her best to fight the feeling. Her right leg started shaking really fast. It was like time was repeating the same exact second over and over and over again just so she could build her fury. Calia slapped her right arm down on her leg. She shook herself and closed her eyes. Not this time. She didn't care what or who Orcon was. He was going to hear her.

"No." Calia said looking down.

"But Calia--"

"I said NO." She raised her head.

"Calia...do you know how much I had to--"

"Mr. Jessley. I am saying this as clear and as nicely as I can. No." Calia responded in a low tone.

"You don't see how--"

"Yes," she started after standing up and looking up to Orcon in his deep and dark eyes, "I do see. Believe me I see clearly. I see that you are scared, and you want me to the cape that saves you. But I will not be. Do I appreciate how you protected me? Yes. Do I know that you are the Alpha and Omega to what I know is my calling? Absolutely. But no. I am not your puppet. I am not your flunkie. And I'm not your Incredible Hulk that will go around making people kill themselves just so you can win a campaign. I will no longer let this keep me from speaking the truth. Speaking MY truth. And if I lose my job because I told you no, then I rather be working at McDonald's asking people if they want fries with their Big Mac than work for you." A silence filled the air after Calia finished. The sound of the air conditioner reminded them they were still on earth, in a house, and looking at each other. Orcon finally blinked and nodded his head.

"Ok." He responded quietly.

Calia's leg stopped shaking. Her body temperature started to decrease as her heart beat went back to its regular speed. She felt tears coming out of her eyes as she closed her eyelids and exhaled.

"Thank you for understanding. I hope I still have my position, but I understand if--"

"You still have your job, Calia. I just realized that I've spent years trying to live down my truth. Move forward from who I am. In truth, who I am is how I got to this point. My dad. He's the reason I've been so successful. I know how it feels to have to be silent. It eats at you. Damn near kills you. And you've probably felt like that for a while. I think it's time I do the same."

"It's something both of us have to get used to. Hell I just learned how to attempt to do it a couple of days ago. But it's possible. We just have to know that our pain is our true power. Mr. J, you can win this election without me. You are an awesome boss and a great person. Your dad really did do a great job. Show people that. That is what is needed in Dallas today."

"I can definitely work on that. Thank you, Ms. LaCaze."

"Most welcome. You hungry?"

"Wait...what?"

"My grandpa is not going to let you leave until you eat, so you might as well go wash your hands, Mr. Millionaire."

"Y'all finished in there? I'm hungry!" Novi shouted from the kitchen.

"We good, Novi. Let's eat!" Calia said.

"I think I'll just be heading out." Orcon answered.

"No you will not," Blaine said coming in from outside.

"Sit down at the table. Future mayors have to eat

too."

"See? Told you." Calia answered with a smile.

CHAPTER 30

"You can't see that illegal screen?" Blaine shouted at the TV. He was watching the New Orleans Pelicans get thrashed by the Miami Heat.

"I can't. Let me take my ass to sleep." he said out loud to the walls. He turned the TV off and headed to the bed. Calia was out with Novi again, and she had her key. He smiled when he thought about those two together. It reminded him of his courtship with Della when they were younger. He turned off the lamp by the recliner. Then, he turned it back on. He looked around to make sure no one was in the house, but he swore someone was watching him. He turned the lamp back off, looked behind him to see nothing, and headed back to his room. He stripped to his boxers and undershirt and nestled under the covers. That same feeling came over him...like he wasn't alone. He heightened his hearing sense to hear footsteps outside his window.

BAM!

The window panes on the left and right side of his bed bust and two men jumped through.

"Move and you die." One of the men shouted. Blaine remained calm on the bed under the covers.

"Look...I don't have anything but take what you want. I'll fix the windows tomor--" The men picked him up out of bed and started to tie him up. Then, they duct taped his mouth shut. Blaine didn't argue. He didn't even fight. The men took him out of the house, placed him in an all-black truck, and drove away.

* * *

"Now explain to me how you know Outkast, but you have never listened to a Goodie Mob album!" Novi asked, parking the car in front of Blaine's house.

"I know. I know. I mean Gnarls Barkley's albums are amazing and--" Calia stopped when Novi's eyes had a sense of concern in them. "Novi? What's wrong?"

"Look for yourself." Novi replied. Calia turned toward her grandfather's house to see the door wide open.

"What the hell?" Calia screamed. She hopped out of the car and ran into the house. The house carpet and floor from Grandpa's room all the way to the front door was messed up."

"Grandpa?!" Calia screamed. She ran to his room. The windows in the room were shattered and there was glass everywhere.

"Calia!" Novi shouted. She followed his voice to her room. "Look at this." Novi said. He handed her the letter.

342-332-3458 FOR BLAINE

She sat on the bed and called the number from her phone. It rang twice before a deep male voice answered.

"Calia. A pleasure to hear from you."

"Who is this?"

"No one important. Your grandfather, however, is very important."

"Where is he?!"

"He's fine...for now. Check your messages. Meet us by 12 PM or you can pick up his dead body."

Click. Calia held the phone looking at it in a daze.

"Calia? Calia? What happened?"

"I...They...got Blaine. I got until 12 PM to meet them or he dies. What is going on?"

"What do you want to do?" Novi asked. Calia's phone alerted her of a text message.

61 PARK COURT. 12 PM. FIND THE BLACK TRUCK.

CHAPTER 31

"How was your stay, Mr. Jessley?" The guest service clerk asked slyly.

"I enjoyed the southern hospitality." Orcon answered, flashing his beautiful million-dollar smile.

"We hope to see you again around here. Take care." She answered slowly, handing him his credit card back. He smiled and turned to head back to his car. His phone rang. *Emmett? Calling me on his off day?*

"Hey E. Everything ok?"

"I wish I could say that. Check your email." Emmett answered. Orcon went to his email on his phone. He opened the unread message Emmett forwarded to him. It was a spreadsheet of this month's spending. $2 million was missing.

"How could Maze miss this?" Orcon asked.

"Did he miss it? That's the real question." Emmett answered.

"Aw shit...not again. Let me deal with this. Thanks

E." Orcon hung up and immediately dialed Maze. It went straight to voicemail. He called again. Voicemail. He hung up and shook his head. He remembered when he was Director of Operations how Maze had trouble with finances to where Cade had to help him handle his gambling problem. Against his better judgement, he kept Maze in that position knowing he could relapse. *Fuck!* Orcon told his car right before the phone rang again. It was a number he didn't recognize.

"Hello?"

"Mr. J. It's Calia. They took him!"

"Took who?"

"My Grandpa Blaine! I don't' know where he's a--"

"Breathe Calia. Breathe. What happened?"

"I got back to my grandpa's house. The door was open. I went to his room and he was not there! The glass was broken too! They left a note for me to call one of them and they told me this address to go to."

"Give me the address." Orcon demanded.

CHAPTER 32

Jo Ann. Thomas. Please let my grandpa be alive. Please. Calia whispered to herself. Her and Novi pulled up to the location. Orcon wasn't far after them. They arrived at a disheveled rice mill trying to remember the good ol' days when it provided millions of people with plates of etouffee and jambalaya. Footsteps crunched as they walked into the open-air way to find Blaine tied to a chair. He looked when he heard footsteps.

"Grandpa!" Calia screamed running towards him.

"Touch him and y'all will see if heaven exists together." Chance said coming out of the shadows. The laser points on his guns were pointed at Calia and Blaine's hearts.

"Chance? What the hell are you doing here?" Orcon asked.

"Ask your friend." Chance gestured his head to the other side of the open space to reveal Maze holding a gun and slightly shaking.

"Maze? This is where you are? Stealing money and

trying to kill people?" Orcon asked.

"No. I'm just trying to kill you. I'm sick of you always taking from me. My hard-earned money. What...what makes you think you have the right to take from me what I've earned? I thought exposing you for who your family is would make you realize differently, but I guess it didn't."

"Like you just took $2 million...again? Still writing checks your gambling can't cash, huh?" Orcon asked.

"They would cash just fine if you would give us what's ours instead of donating to some whack ass charity that won't help no damn body. A measly $2 mil is not going to help nobody in Oak Cliff!"

"Wow. You are...just...ok. Cade was right. Trying to help you is pointless." Orcon answered.

"Uh...are you two done with your bromance? I got shit to do." Chance interrupted.

"Hold on Maze. Calia needs to know the truth. She needs to know that her money is being given to a charity that may disappear in who knows how long. She may want her raise. Don't you want your raise?" Maze asked.

"I want my grandfather, and I'm asking nicely for you to let him go." Calia demanded.

"We will. As soon as we get what we need from you too. "Maze said with a smile. A loud ZOOP streaked passed Calia's ear.

"Ugh!"

Calia turned around. Novi was grabbing his chest as he fell to the ground.

"NOOOOOOOO!" Calia screamed. She ran and fell to her knees holding his chest with him. Novi heaved and heaved. Blood started to drip from his lip. "Novi? Novi. Stay with me. Please. Hold on. Please." Novi continued to attempt to breathe, but she felt his breath slowly fade away until he took his final heave and stopped.

"Did she have to scream that loud?" Chance asked sarcastically.

Calia felt her entire body go numb. Her body temperature rose. She slowly moved her head up. She stared at Chance. He held this incredibly stupid smile on his face. Then, she shot over to Maze. Her eyes locked directly on him. His body froze. Then, he turned toward Chance. Shots rang like church bells as Maze emptied the entire gun clip into Chance's body. Chance convulsed and flailed until he finally fell to the ground. Red streams oozed out of his body creating a circular puddle of blood that mimicked red Kool aid with too much sugar. His body laid lifeless with eyes open and his mouth agape.

Maze brought his arms down to his sides. He blinked really hard and shook his head. He looked over to see Chance riddled with bullets.

"Did I..." He started to ask. He turned his head toward Calia to see her staring at her with death in her eyes and tears streaming down her cheeks. Orcon moved slowly toward Maze, but it was too late. Maze was running out of the mill trying to get to his car.

Orcon picked up one of Chance's guns and ran after him. Maze shot bullets towards him hoping to give himself time, but this wasn't Orcon's first encounter with guns. He ducked and dodged until he finally got outside.

"Maze!" Orcon screamed. He got outside to see Maze holding up the gun toward his head.

"Don't. You. Move. Calia or no Calia, I will light your ass up out here without a second thought." Maze said nervously.

Orcon stood ready to draw his gun but decided instead to slowly put his gun on the ground. Then, he stood up and placed his hands behind his back. Orcon remembered faces from his past that looked exactly like Maze's face.

"A second thought, huh? Hmm. Ok. You know...it was my dad, Royalty, that taught me to keep your friends close but your enemies closer. I guess I did that part right. But he also taught me that a person who wants to kill doesn't wait to pull the trigger. They do it. That's why my dad is no longer here. So, if you really wanted me dead, you would have shot me the moment I got here. That shaking you doing also tells me you are not ready to do what a real man would. Put the gun down, Maze, and save yourself the embarrassment."

"No. No! You are the reason I'm in this shit! If you would have just..."

"Just what? Not be me? I'm sorry but Royalty didn't raise me that way. I do what I have to do by any means necessary. Can you say the same?"

"Shut up O!"

"For what? Am I saying something wrong? Shoot me. I'm right here. Pull the trigger."

Maze's finger started to press the trigger until it froze. His fingers moved off the trigger. Then, his whole arm started to slowly move to where the gun was on his right thigh. Then, the gun went off.

"Ahhh!" Maze screamed. Orcon turned around to see Blaine staring directly at Maze. Maze moved to his other thigh and shot himself again. Then, each finger slowly released itself from the gun. Maze's body started to crawl into a ball as he screamed in agony. Orcon moved slowly toward Maze. He picked up the gun.

"A boy can't do a man job, Maze." Orcon said. He walked away. Maze laid on the ground shaking and looking up at the sky while blood seeped out of his legs.

CHAPTER 33

Blue and red lights bounced off the metal walls of the old rice mill. Cancel P.D. brought 5 cars, 1 ambulance, and 1 coroner to investigate, clean up, and question. As Maze was put onto a stretcher and pushed into the ambulance, Calia hung her head and closed her eyes. She thought about the fact that she had a hand in taking the lives of two people: one when she could not control it and one she chose. Was she wrong? Could she have done something different? Then, she thought about Novi. His smile. His arms. His conversation. She will never have it again with him. Memories will have to keep her fed and watered.

"Grandpa?"

"Yes, baby?"

"How do you deal with...you know...the effects?"

Blaine nodded his head. "I felt how you did when I couldn't control. I felt like I had to pay a price for having this gift. And I did. Plenty of times. But I also looked at what I gained once I learned how to handle it. I gained understanding. Patience. Timing. Self-Control. I can't tell you what will happen for you. I do know that when you find it, whatever it is, it will be exactly what you need for who you are."

Calia repeated his last words in her mind hoping it would stick. She wasn't entirely ok, but she looked forward to when she would be.

"Thank you Blaine." Orcon stated.

"Thank you. Your dad would be mighty proud of you."

"That's the hope. Are you going to be ok, Calia?" Orcon asked.

"We'll see. That's the hope. Thank you for coming back." Calia responded.

"I'm glad I did. I'm sorry you got tangled up in this. I can't believe I trusted him. My instincts are usually way better than this."

"Some people live to be snakes in the grass. At least you found out before you got bit." Blaine explained.

"Understood. Definitely understood now. I better head back to Dallas and start damage control. Take two weeks to get things together down here. I'll explain to Drame what's going on." Orcon stated.

"Thank you. I'm going to need it." Calia answered. She and Blaine watched as Orcon got into his car and headed home.

Chapter 34

"Well...I'm headed back. I...uh...took some of your paintings. I hope you don't mind. I need to remember who set the precedence for a good boyfriend. Oh. I brought you this." Calia placed Usher's *My Way* CD on Novi's grave. "I hope God will let you listen to it. Usher was kind of suggestive for his young age. Good...but suggestive. Anyway, make sure you find my mom and grandma. They will take care of you. I...I love you. Be easy, homie." Calia walked away slowly with tears flowing down her face. She got into Blaine's truck and opened the glove compartment for tissues.

"Ok," she told Blaine, "Let's go." He put his truck into gear and drove away from West Cancel Cemetery. They stopped at the Shop Quick right before the interstate. Calia went in to pay for gas. While waiting in line, a huge burly white man stepped in front of her.

"Excuse me. I was here first." Calia stated politely.

"Ok?" He said with an attitude.

"Can you please move to the back of the line?"

"You need to be back there anyway, little girl." Calia

took a deep breath in and then let it out. "Let it go, Calia. Let it go." She said out loud to herself. When the white man got to the counter, the white woman cashier looked at him crazy. "Uh...sir...you need to go to the back of the line."

"For what?"

"Because she was here first."

"What difference does it make? I'm here now."

"Well you will not be leaving with any of our merchandise if you don't move to the back of the line." The cashier answered. The white man dropped all his items and walked out the store cursing and shouting. Calia moved up to the counter.

"Thank you." Calia stated.

The cashier winked. "Anytime sweetheart. Assholes like that need to learn a lesson."

Calia paid for her items and walked back to the car where Blaine was waiting.

"Here is your 7UP, Grandpa." Calia handed Blaine the soda.

"Thank you ma'am." Blaine answered.

"Ready to go?" Calia said.

"Yep. It's time for Dallas to meet all the LaCaze's." Blaine answered. Blaine started the car. The radio was blasting Sly and the Family Stone. They started nodding their heads on the same beat as Sly.

Thank you for letting me be myself again...
I wanna thank you for letting me be myself again...

EPILOGUE

Ain't No Stopping Us Now
We're on the move!
Ain't No Stopping Us Now
We've got the groove!

"Alright Na!" Blaine shouted while moving to the beat while dancing with Calia. The Renaissance ballroom was filled with workers and supporters waiting for the results of the Mayor of Dallas candidate race. Orcon moved around the crowd smiling and shaking hands. He stood back when he saw Blaine busting a move.

"Ok, Mr. LaCaze!" He said joyfully.

"Don't let this salt and pepper beard fool y'all." Blaine answered.

"Breathe, Mr. J. Either way, you ran a great campaign. The least you can do is dance and look silly with us while waiting." Calia explained. Orcon joined them as they danced to the music.

"Mr. Jessley?" Tress interrupted, "They are about to announce the winners."

"Well, duty calls." Orcon said. He followed Tress to the big screen where BREAKING NEWS appeared on the screen.

"With 98% of the precincts in Dallas reporting, the winner of the mayoral election is Edgar Campbell!" Orcon's eyes softened as everyone expressed their disgust and disapproval. Orcon, however, smiled as he prepared to go and face reporters. Before he went to meet the reporter mob, he went to find two people: Ms. Merry and Mama Janice. His visit to Louisiana made him realize how much God never let him go without a mother in his life. He found them sitting at a table talking to each other.

"Ladies?" He said, holding out his hands.

"Where we goin'? We were having a good conversation about *The Price Is Right!*" Ms. Merry asked. Orcon shook his head as they took his hands. They moved in sync all the way to the ballroom's main doors. Camera flashes and jumbles of questioning met Orcon. He held up his hand to ask for silence.

"First, I would like to thank everyone who helped me on this journey. It was not an easy experience, but you stuck by my side even when I didn't know what would happen next. Second, I want to congratulate Mayor Campbell on his win. I pray that you remember the eminence this city holds, and I am here to help in any way I can to perpetuate that greatness. Finally...I have to apologize. For the longest I have tried to run away from who I really am. I created this persona that would lead you to believe I am just a hard-working kid from Oak Cliff. I'm not. I am the son of a drug kingpin and a crackhead. I am from a small town that barely has a stoplight. I am from living from paycheck to paycheck but working hard for it...even if it was illegal. My name is Magic. Magic Calhoune. Royalty's son. Owner of the Dallas Leopards. And forever a lover of the great city of Dallas. And as much as I want to answer your questions, I rather dance and enjoy tonight with two of the prettiest young women here." Magic reached for the hands of Ms. Merry and Mama Janice. "Good night." He turned around and headed to the dance floor. While dancing with them, he looked up to the ceiling. *We'll be back Dad...by any means necessary.*

Get connected with Author J.W. Bella on social media

JW Bella

jwbellawrites

jwbellawrites

OTHER BOOKS BY THIS AUTHOR

If you are an author looking for a great place to promote your book and expand your audience join the Sign My Book family. Submit your request at www.jwbellawrites.com/sign-my-book-podcast.

CPSIA information can be obtained
at www.ICGtesting.com
Printed in the USA
FSHW011344300621